To Joy,

THE MAKING OF A SMALL-TOWN
Beauty King

Savy Leiser (signature)

SAVY LEISER

Dedicated to my partner, Tyler,
My brother, Ross,
And our friends, Jason and Sean,
Because of that one time in high school when we
made a really big trebuchet and used it to fling
stuff everywhere.
That was fun.

CONTENTS

Chapter One
Sunday

Hard work. Hard work and just being a nice guy. Isn't that what it's all about? Also, the hokey pokey. Scratch. *I first learned the value of hard work at a young age. Six, when I earned my first dollar. It was for unclogging my grandpa's toilet. Looking back, I was undervaluing my services.* Scratch.

Jackie Almond sighed and crossed out another line of writing in his notebook. Underneath the "College Essay" heading at the top, the entire page was covered in the dark blue ink of words crossed out. It was less than an hour until closing at Almond's Convenience Store, which meant Jackie could take his focus away from the overwhelming lack of customers in front of him at the cash register, and instead put his focus on his overwhelming lack of college essay topics.

Self-reflection. Something I first truly experienced after reading The Catcher in the Rye. *What a book. I was never the same.* SCRATCH.

"Excuse me, son?" A low, rumbly voice penetrated Jackie's concentration, not that he minded. He looked up to see an obese, balding man with an abundance of arm hair and a lime-green polo tucked into his khakis standing before him. This, plus his wimpy comb-over and overpowering scent of discount cologne all combined to make him exactly the type of customer Jackie was expecting. "I'd like to buy one of these." Jackie watched as the man placed a copy of the *Grey Acres Gazette* on the counter. The front-page headline, "94th Annual Town Fair Comes to Grey Acres," stared up at him.

"Fifty cents. Anything else?"

He stared straight into Jackie's eyes. "Well, you know, I *wanted* a sandwich from the deli." A moment of silence slowly passed, the man never breaking eye contact.

Jackie drew a deep breath, preparing himself for the argument he knew was coming. There was one almost every shift. "I'm sorry, sir. The deli closes at nine."

"I *know* the deli closes at nine. Why don't you think I have a sandwich?" The man even cocked his head a little for dramatic effect.

"Oh, uh, I'm sorry—"

"People are still hungry after nine, you know. The human body doesn't magically stop metabolizing just because it's nine o'clock." His hands gestured wildly, especially around the word "magically."

Jackie blinked. "I understand that. That's why we've got snacks, you know, like chips and stuff—"

"I don't want chips and stuff. I want a sandwich."

Jackie stared at the man for a moment. He blinked again. "The newspaper's fifty cents."

Ten p.m. couldn't come fast enough. After the man strutted out of the store, frustratedly swinging the newspaper at his side, Jackie spent the rest of the hour dividing his attention between his nonexistent college essay and the second hand of his watch. As soon as ten o'clock hit, Jackie started unpinning his nametag, his jittery fingers fumbling with the same rush of excitement he felt every night.

"It's ten, Dad!" Jackie shouted from the register.

His father, Jack Almond Sr., poked his head out from the Employees Only door, his hair greasy with Rogaine and a hard day's work. "Flip the sign on your way out," he called.

Jackie stuffed his nametag in his pocket and headed for the door, flipping the hanging sign to the "Closed" side on his way out and pulling his cell phone out of his jeans pocket. After sending a quick text to his best friend, Logan Feinstein, saying that he'd be on the roof in just a sec, he walked out the door, past the neon-red flickering "Convenience Store" sign, and over to a ladder on the side of the building.

He climbed the ladder until he reached the roof, where he found Logan waiting for him the same way he was every night: lying on his back, holding some sort of reading material above his head. Tonight, it was the *Grey Acres Gazette*.

The roof of Almond's Convenience Store had been Jackie and Logan's special meeting place ever since Jackie had started working there about two years ago, the day after his sixteenth birthday. Sixteen was the legal working age in Grey Acres, but Jack Sr. thought it would be rude to request that Jackie start working *on* his birthday, so he waited until the day after to employ him. Of course, he couldn't resist giving Jackie his convenience store nametag in a Fine Jewelry box as one of his birthday gifts. Jackie found the gag a weird mix of kinda-funny and kinda-frustrating. It was like the feeling he got when he ate mediocre pizza or dark chocolate. A little pleasure with a little disappointment.

Maybe the nametag in a gift box is a metaphor for my life, thought Jackie, before filing it away in his brain as a possible college essay topic, then taking a seat cross-legged on the roof next to Logan.

"Did you see the headline on page three?" Logan asked, rocking his body forward to sit up.

"I've started actively avoiding reading the newspapers at this point," said Jackie.

"'Local Grey Acres Woman Teaches Cat to Fertilize Mushrooms.' Fascinating."

"And to think. Every other customer who came in today will be reading this story tonight."

"You think the cat shits on the mushrooms himself, or what?"

Jackie shrugged, nodding.

Jackie and Logan had been best friends since before kindergarten. Back in the early 2000s, Jack Almond Sr. and Logan's dad, Ronald Feinstein, would go to meetings of the Midwest Small Business Owners' Society together, Jack for his convenience store and Ronald for his department store at the Grey Acres Mall. Because of that, the two of them were always meeting up for lunch to discuss their businesses, or "talk shop" as they called it, and sometimes brought little Jackie and little Logan along with them. Jackie and Logan would spend those afternoons crawling under tables at restaurants or drawing on tablecloths in crayon, whispering to each other about how "talking shop makes daddies boring."

Of course, this meant that when Jackie and Logan started school at Grey Acres Elementary, they already had each other as a best friend, and it just kind of naturally stayed that way.

"Speaking of breaking news," said Logan, his voice muffled by a loud rustling as he turned a page in the newspaper, "I heard through the grapevine that Erin's planning to ask me out to the Town Fair this Saturday."

"Oooh. Logan's got a daaaate."

"To the *fair*. It's like, 'Ooh, look at this award-winning tomato, honey. It's red and juicy just like my heart. And this second-place pumpkin is round and firm like your body.' How romantic."

"*Second*-place pumpkin?"

Logan's eyes didn't look up from the newspaper. "I'm aiming low to avoid disappointment. Besides, who even brings dates to the fair anymore? I should be like, 'Hey, Erin. 1962 called. It wants to ask you on a date to the fair.'"

Back in middle school, Jackie and Logan were the infamous duo who took girls out on double dates together, usually to a school dance or the Grey Acres Mall, and usually breaking it off after one or two dates. It wasn't their fault, though; Grey Acres Junior High dances and the Grey Acres Mall were, for the most part, barren, pathetic date spots. Not even a Shakespearean couple could fall in love there, unless they were a Shakespearean couple with a fetish for places that hadn't been renovated since the early 80s. Jackie and Logan managed to keep this routine up through the beginning of their sophomore year of high school when, out of nowhere, Logan started to show a sharp decline in his interest in girls, and a sharp, *sharp* increase in his interest in books. Jackie thought this was kinda lame at first, but within a few months, he had a job at his dad's store thrust upon him, and his dating life saw an unintentional plummet as well. Yet, even when both of them had both time and an interested pair of girls on their side, Logan showed little to no interest, which disappointed Jackie until he found out why.

Jackie chuckled at Logan's produce analogy. "We're talking about Aaron here, right? Tall Aaron who always wears those funky little bow ties?"

"Nope. Erin with an E."

"Oh. Sorry, bud."

Logan sighed. "Like I'd get a date with Aaron with an A. That'd be the day, right?"

"I dunno," Jackie said, shrugging. "Anything's possible."

"Grey Acres isn't ready for that kinda thing yet."

"Grey Acres is still fascinated by a cat taking a dump on fungus. I really wouldn't take it personally."

Logan laughed. "Yeah, I guess you're right."

A moment of silence followed, leaving Jackie and Logan looking out at the town of Grey Acres, or as much of it as they could see from a one-story convenience store roof. Past the store's parking lot stretched a few acres of empty grass that no one ever bothered to use for their intended agricultural purposes. In just six days, the annual Town Fair would be set up there, turning an empty field of crunchy, puke-colored, brownish-green grass into an elaborate setup of white tents and wooden stages. Off in the distance, they could see the faint outline of Grey Acres High School, lit up by the street lamps around it. To their left, they saw the town's only notable restaurant, a combination Crunchy's Chicken and Paul's Pancake World, as well as a dimly lit Gus's Supermarket. Logan was always annoyed that the supermarket's owner, Gus Bennett, didn't name the store Gus's Groceries. It was a painful waste of alliteration, and Logan knew that, if it weren't the only grocery store in town, Gus would be missing out on some serious marketing opportunities. To their right, Jackie and Logan saw a few houses haphazardly placed throughout the fields, without any real order or system. Jackie always theorized that John Greyacres, or whatever the original Grey Acres city planner's name was, just decided to vomit all over a giant piece of paper, and wherever the biggest chunks landed, that's where he put houses. It made more sense than any other system. The house with the largest field around it held Simon's Pumpkin Farm, the family-owned pumpkin business that dominated the produce-growing competitions at the fair every year. Jackie and Logan both sighed. Trying to take in all of Grey Acres at once always proved disappointing.

"Man, I am *so* glad I'm getting out of this town," said Logan. "I submitted six more applications today. Last month was NYU and UCLA, and then today was UChicago, USC—"

"Oh *shit*!" Jackie snapped out of his trance. "I totally forgot. I gotta meet with *Flounder* tomorrow."

Chapter Two

Monday

Jackie sat slumped over in his chair, rhythmically drumming his fingers on his knees. Every few seconds, he looked up to see his guidance counselor, Marvin Flounder, sorting through the mountain of manila folders on his desk, stopping every so often to inhale with an obnoxious *snort*. Marvin Flounder was the kind of man who proudly sported a balding head with pre-cancerous sunspots, a bushy black mustache, and Coke-bottle glasses, and who treated motivational posters from Target as if they were wallpaper. Jackie's eyes darted to the poster placed directly behind Flounder's desk, which featured a neon-yellow smiley face surrounded by a circle of Comic Sans text: "Shoot for the moon! If you miss, you might just land in Mr. Flounder's office!"

"Jackson Almond!" Flounder's painfully nasal voice boomed, as he slammed a manila folder down on top of his folder mountain.

"You know I go by Jackie, right?"

"Yes, Jackson, but this morning I read in a poll that most colleges dislike gender neutral names. I'm doing you a favor."

"Well, then I'd hate to be a Jamie. Or a Taylor. Or James Taylor. Not because of the name, just because his music's kinda boring."

Flounder made a dramatic show of rolling his eyes, so much that his head even rolled around a little bit. He then opened Jackie's manila folder and flipped through the pages. "Cornell, I see? And with Michigan as your second choice. I guess we're aiming high, aren't we, Jackson? Shooting for the *moooooon*?"

Jackie watched the little black eyes on the smiley face above Flounder's desk as they stared into his soul. "Well, yeah. I mean, I'm gonna be the first one in my family to go to college, so I figured, might as well go all out."

"Mmmm *hmmmmm*," Flounder's piercingly nasal voice vibrated. "And what is it you're planning to study?"

"I mean, I guess I've always liked a little of everything," Jackie said, shrugging. "Maybe start off with some history, have a little English, some math on the side. You know, like a big educational buffet."

"*Interesting.* I thought that spending so much time with that Logan Feinstein would have given you some focus. I received notice that, so far, he's applied to eight English programs, *three* of them Ivies."

"Isn't it like, illegal for you to reveal that information or something? Like, isn't there some sort of counselor-student confidentiality clause?"

Flounder rolled his eyes again, this time punctuating his eye-roll with one of his *snort*s. "I'm being *serious,* Jackson."

Jackie, who had been being serious as well, took a moment to appreciate that he'd never felt any desire to share any of his personal problems with Flounder.

"So," Flounder continued, "*No* idea what you want to study? At *all*?"

"I mean..." Jackie looked around the room, hoping a motivational poster might give him the answer Flounder wanted. "I guess not. Isn't part of college, like, finding yourself? Learning your 'purpose' and all that existential stuff?"

"Look, you don't seem to get it, so I'll just give it to you straight. Your grades are good... ish. Your SAT is *slightly* above average, but without a passion, or without something you excel at, what's setting you apart from every other competent kid that applies? Nothing, Jackson. You have *nothing*."

Jackie froze for a moment, realizing he'd never been given anything that straight before. He always knew he wasn't quite as smart as Logan, but then again, most kids weren't. He was used to regular compliments from his dad on his work ethic, including a few employee-of-the-month awards at the convenience store, which he was promised every time were free of nepotism. But, it was turning out, most college-bound kids were hard workers. "I guess I could have my essay," Jackie finally answered. "I'd stand out to them if I wrote a really kick-ass essay, right?"

Flounder glared at Jackie and pointed to a motivational poster hanging on the wall to Jackie's left. It featured a fuzzy brown teddy bear with a bar of soap jammed in its mouth, accompanied by text reading, "Watch your language, kids."

"A kick... rear-end essay?" Jackie offered.

"Very good. Now, what do you plan to write about?"

Jackie reviewed his list of failed essay topics from the night before. There was only one he hadn't yet attempted. "Well, I was thinking, how about my dad, Jack Almond Sr.? Great guy. Grew up in poverty, beat cancer twice, eventually achieved his goal of owning his own convenience store." Hearing himself say it out loud, Jackie realized that he actually kind of liked the idea. "And the reason he *wanted* the store was to make enough money to send his kids to college one day. And then from there, I'd lead into why I want to go to college. You know. Heartwarming and shit." Jackie's eyes darted back to the poster. "I mean... and feces."

Flounder blinked. "Who's applying to Cornell? You, or your dad?"

"I mean, *I* am, though I can't say he'd *never* want to try going back to school—"

"Then why are you trying to impress them with how great someone *else* is? What have *you* accomplished? What is *your* purpose?"

Jackie opened his mouth, ready to answer. But as nothing came out, he realized he didn't have anything to say. And he doubted any of Flounder's posters could help him with that.

Flounder's words lingered in Jackie's head for the rest of the day, annoying him as he went from class to class, even following him home. That night, Jackie sat at the dinner table, lost in thought, as his mother served dinner.

As Jackie stared off into space, Heather Almond, still wearing a dark-green Almond's Convenience Store apron, spooned leftover mac n' cheese from last night's dinner at Crunchy's onto three plates. Jackie's trance was suddenly shattered when his eight-year-old brother, Terry, piped up, "No vegetables today, Mom?"

"What, are you sad about that or something?" Heather asked, setting down the bowl and sitting in her chair. "Since when do *you* want vegetables?"

"¡Como *siempre*, Mamasita!" Terry exclaimed.

"Jackie, since when does your brother like vegetables?"

"Oh. I think he's been studying them for the vegetable growing contest at the fair. Right, buddy?"

"¡Sí!" Terry shouted, throwing his arms in the air.

"And since when does he speak Spanish?" Heather asked.

Jackie chuckled. "Terry, have you been watching the Spanish channel again?"

"Sí, para las *mujeres*," Terry replied with a wink.

Heather stared at Jackie, mouthing, "What does that mean?" Jackie shrugged.

"It means *for the ladies*," Terry explained matter-of-factly.

"You oughta go easy on the telenovelas, buddy," Jackie said.

"Las telenovelas son bonitas," Terry replied.

"So, Jackie, how did your meeting with Mr. Flounder go today?" Heather asked, looking to change the subject.

"It went fine," said Jackie. "But I was wondering. What do you think is my purpose in life?"

"Excuse me?"

"Like… why am I here?"

"Well," Heather explained, "back in the 90s I met a nice young man named Jack Almond Sr., and we loved each other *very* much—"

"Mom, are you *sure* you wanna have this conversation with an eight-year-old at the table?"

"Lighten up, Jackie," Terry said through a mouthful of mac n' cheese. He swallowed with a big *gulp*. "After all, *I'm* the one who's full of love for *las mujeres*."

Even Terry's passionate about something, Jackie thought to himself. "What do you guys think I'm passionate about?" he asked.

Heather glanced at her watch. "If you have any sense, you'll be passionate about getting yourself to work in twenty minutes. Dad called earlier and said he wants you to run the deli tonight."

Jackie sighed. Of all the things he might be passionate about, running the deli definitely wasn't one of them.

Twenty minutes later, Jackie stood behind a counter featuring a smorgasbord of meats and cheeses, wrapping finished sandwiches in aluminum foil and putting them on the counter for customers.

"How's it going, Jackie?" a girl's voice asked, getting closer to him with every syllable.

Jackie looked up to see Stephanie Simon, heiress to Simon's Pumpkin Farm, in old faded jeans and a navy blue Mathletes sweatshirt, approaching the counter. She was accompanied by her mother, Debra, who wore a baggy flannel shirt and dirty workboots. "Oh, hey, Steph," said Jackie.

Steph hungrily eyed the meats. "Did you finish Mr. Kowalski's history paper yet?"

"Nah, not yet. I'm still working on the thesis—"

"We're kind of in a hurry," Debra interrupted, her voice short and curt. "Bowl of vegetable soup to go." She even snapped her fingers.

Jackie, a little taken aback by Debra's rudeness, turned to a steaming metal pot next to the meats and ladled some soup into a Styrofoam bowl. He placed it on the counter, all the while avoiding eye contact with Debra.

"I'm feeling a foot-long Italian sub," Steph said. "Extra Provolone. Maybe some mayo—"

"Just one of these for Stephanie," Debra declared, holding up a clear plastic to-go box of green salad. She shook it around so the lettuce loudly rattled against the plastic, an alternative to her finger-snapping.

Steph rolled her eyes and continued talking as if Debra weren't there. "And some lettuce, tomato, onion... do you have chipotle sauce?"

"Stephanie, I don't have time for this," Debra interjected. "And the pageant's this Saturday, so neither do you, if you know what I mean."

The Grey Acres Beauty Pageant was always a central event at the Town Fair, right up there with the vegetable contests. Every year, girls aged fourteen to eighteen got all dolled up to make speeches that were somewhere between suck-uppy and sarcastic about how much they loved the town of Grey Acres, and what being Fair Queen would mean to them. Jackie knew a lot about the pageant, since almost every girl he'd ever taken on a date in the early fall would gush about how she hoped she'd be Fair Queen that year. He never quite knew why. The Fair Queen title didn't come with any kind of cash prize as far as he knew, nor was it affiliated with any other beauty pageants in any way. Jackie had always figured the real prize of the title was probably the bragging rights that came along with it, something about the ego boost that came with being the prettiest girl in the shittiest town. None of his dates ever ended up winning, as far as he remembered.

Stephanie finally turned her gaze away from the sandwich toppings to stare Debra in the eye. "No, I don't. What *do* you mean?"

Debra sighed and exasperatedly rubbed her temples. "I already let you have the big Thermos of mac n' cheese for lunch, okay? *Don't* push me on this whole sandwich thing."

"Are you saying I'm *fat*?" Steph asked. Debra rolled her eyes in lieu of answering. "Because I've calculated it, Mom. My weight is in the 30th percentile for my age. That's *average*. Or, I guess, it's the *median*, since there are always statistical outliers—"

"Oh, come *on*, Stephanie. Do *not* do that math stuff to me."

"That math stuff? Wow. I'm done." Steph turned her head and looked Jackie in the eye. "Jackie, make the sandwich."

Jackie looked to the meats in front of him, then up at Steph and Debra. A long line was growing behind them, full of customers tapping their feet and impatiently staring at their watches.

Steph pulled a crumpled five-dollar bill out of her sweatshirt pocket and waved it in front of him. "Jackie, I'm a paying customer. Sandwich."

Jackie grabbed a twelve-inch roll and rapidly started sawing it in half. After the bread was cut, he opened it and started frantically piling slices of salami on top.

"Stop making the sandwich. We're not paying for that," said Debra. "Stephanie, I've told you a million times you can't afford to eat like that right now."

"And I've told *you* a million times I'm not entering that pageant," Steph argued.

As Jackie nervously threw Provolone at the bread and haphazardly squirted mayo out of a plastic bottle, he heard customers starting to make remarks off in the distance.

"What's the hold up?"

"Just order your goddamn food."

"Women. Always holding up the line with their chit-chat."

"Jack *Sr.* would have never let this happen."

Steph stared daggers at Debra. "That pageant objectifies women, *Mom*."

Jackie tossed the sandwich in the oven and stealthily wiped a bit of sweat from above his eyebrows.

"Objectifies women?" Debra repeated. She turned to Jackie. "I'm sorry. I don't know where she gets this stuff."

"Your soup and salad are on the counter, ma'am," Jackie said, speaking so quickly his words almost ran together. "You may take them to the checkout now."

"I don't 'get this stuff' anywhere. It's obvious. Women being awarded for their looks is sexist," said Steph.

"How is it *sexist*?" Debra asked, her voice growing more exasperated by the second.

"Well, when's the last time you saw a *man* be crowned Fair Queen?"

Jackie froze for a moment. He imagined a teenage boy, with hairy legs and a wispy, undeveloped mustache, wearing an ill-fitting dress that sagged in all the wrong places and standing amidst a group of girls. The boy looked ridiculous. But the boy stood out.

Suddenly, Jackie's daydream was halted by the *ding* of the sandwich oven. He pulled the sandwich out, quickly wrapped it in foil, and threw it on the counter. "There you go, Steph." Steph grabbed the sandwich off the counter and bolted for the checkout, leaving Debra to follow behind her.

"Next!" Jackie called.

Later that night, Steph sat on the old grey couch in her living room, a calculus textbook open in her lap. She rhythmically tapped her pencil against her notebook, trying to focus on the integration problem she was solving. On the cushion next to her sat the tinfoil from her sandwich, open, with half of the sandwich peeking out. Steph picked up the foil and took a bite of the sandwich inside.

She looked to her eight-year-old sister, Lizzie, who was sitting on the floor in front of her. In each hand, Lizzie held a naked Barbie doll. One of the Barbie dolls had half of her head shaved. "Pow!

Pow, pow, pow!" Lizzie screamed, as she made one Barbie slap and headbutt the other. A pile of dead Barbie casualties lay on the floor next to Lizzie.

Debra's footsteps became audible, as she paced back and forth between the hallway and kitchen. Steph stopped tapping her pencil against her notebook to listen, as she could suddenly hear Debra's voice faintly in the distance, talking on the phone.

"I don't want to *push* her or anything," said Debra. "I just want her to have the same experience I had. If she never gets it, she won't know what she's missing out on... Right, I agree. She's too young to realize it, but her glory days won't last forever."

Steph sighed, rolling her eyes. She looked up to the mantel above the fireplace, which housed a row of gold plaques. Amidst various first and second-place pumpkin awards addressed to Simon's Pumpkin Farm, there sat one plaque, slightly larger than all the others, in the middle: Debra Simon, 1989 Grey Acres Fair Queen.

"Sounds like Mom's talking to Aunt Patty again, huh, Lizzie?" said Steph.

"Ka-*POW*!" Lizzie responded, not looking up, as she reached under her pile of dead Barbies and flung them all around the room in a giant doll explosion. "That's why you *don't mess* with Nuclear Barbie," she whispered under her breath.

Steph shook her head, laughing a little. She looked at the family photos nailed to the wall above the plaques. There were a few of Steph, Debra, and Lizzie outside on the pumpkin farm, and a few of the three of them at Christmas time, but the one that stood out was a faded portrait of a teenage Debra, wearing a shiny ivory gown, a silver tiara, and a blue "Fair Queen" sash. Teenage Debra had a dramatically wide, yet somehow genuine looking, smile as she posed with a first-place-winning pumpkin. Steph sighed again and looked out the window. She stared at the Pumpkin Farm, which stretched for acres and acres beyond their house. Most pumpkins were bright orange and perfectly round, but a few were slightly undersized or misshapen, and a few had bruises or mold along the side.

"Like, I *get* that she has these big dreams for college and stuff, and like I *want* to believe in her, and I *do*, to an extent, but... yeah, you know..."

Steph felt her blood pressure rising and her face getting hot with frustration. Debra was always making passive-aggressive comments like that, comments that made her *sound* like she cared about you, without putting in any real effort to do so. Comments like "I *want* to believe in her, *but...*". It was always the *but* that got Steph. Why couldn't her mom just *believe in her*, period? *Periods are better than buts*, thought Steph. She considered filing that phrase away in her mind, on the off chance that some variation of it would make a good slogan for the after-school feminist club she sometimes ran, but quickly realized how few people it would attract.

"Yeah," Debra continued, "I'll have to try to talk her down later. You should've seen her, Patty. She was just making *such a scene*, and for *absolutely no reason at all—*"

Steph bolted up from the couch, slamming her notebook shut. As she quickly gathered her books in her arms, a tri-fold brochure slipped out from between her notebook's pages and fell onto the couch. The words "MIT Math Program" were splashed across the top, with a few college-aged kids standing underneath them holding piles of books and sporting giant smiles. Steph always loved how happy those kids seemed to look just to be holding books on the MIT campus. They gave her hope that one day she'd be that happy too.

As Debra continued her phone conversation with Aunt Patty in the next room, Steph stormed out of the living room and up the stairs, leaving the remaining quarter of her sandwich untouched on the couch. Lizzie looked at the sandwich, still half-wrapped in tin foil, and made her two surviving Barbies attack it like vultures.

Chapter Three

Tuesday

On his way to class Tuesday morning, Logan walked past rows of slightly rusting maroon lockers, eyeing posters advertising the fair crookedly scotch-taped to the walls, and occasionally fielding flirtatious waves from a couple girls with a nonchalant nod. Suddenly, he felt a tug on his backpack, slowing his movement. He turned his head to see Jackie jogging to catch up to him.

"Logan, my man!" Jackie shouted. "I've got it all figured out."

"I'm aware. I got all eight of the texts you sent me while I was asleep telling me you've got it all figured out, you understand your purpose, your life now has meaning, and whatever the other five said. And I'm not gonna lie, you've got me curious, considering yesterday you were having an existential crisis over a meeting with Marvin Flounder."

Jackie swung his arm around Logan's shoulders as they walked down the hall together. "Yesterday was *Monday*, dude. But today is *Tuesday*, and the world is my oyster!"

"Care to elaborate?"

"I found it, man. The thing that's gonna make me stand out. To Flounder, to colleges, *everything*!"

Jackie detached himself from Logan as they approached the door to their first class. He opened the door and the two walked inside.

Jackie and Logan entered Mr. Kowalski's history class, a modest beige room decorated with posters of George Washington, Christopher Columbus, and other clichéd figures from American history. Jackie and Logan found desks next to each other.

Once they were seated, Jackie leaned in and whispered in Logan's ear. "I'm gonna be the 94th annual Grey Acres Fair Queen."

"What?"

"You heard me. I'll dress real pretty, strut down the stage, make a big speech about how much I love this town—"

"But you hate this town."

"Yeah, *everyone* hates this town. But they somehow always have a Fair Queen, don't they? They always manage to find... what is that dumb phrase they use?... *the face of Grey Acres.*"

"Yeah, but I'm not sure if you noticed, that face always happens to be of the female variety."

"That's why this is *brilliant*. The first-ever *male* Fair Queen." Jackie smiled to himself. "The colleges are gonna eat this shit *up.*"

In front of Jackie and Logan sat Steph and her best friend, Erin McCloskey. Erin was a cute girl who gave off a retro vibe, which today consisted of a waist-high tweed pleated skirt, a collared shirt covered by a cashmere sweater, and a blue bow holding up her strawberry-blonde ponytail. Erin and Steph had been naturally drawn to each other when they first met in sixth grade as the only two girls on the Academic Team. They solidified their lifelong best-friendship during one after-school practice when the team captain, Brad Thompson, told Erin he'd make her a starter if she'd just show him her titties, and Steph responded by locking Brad alone in a closet with Helga, the classroom's pet rat. Unfortunately, once ninth grade began, the girls' stint as Academic Team Power Couple had to come to an end, since Grey Acres High School had only a Mathletes team, and Erin was always more of a literature girl.

Upon hearing Jackie and Logan whispering to each other behind them, Steph and Erin turned around in their seats.

"Hey, Jackie, sorry about that whole thing at the deli last night," said Steph.

"Don't you worry about a thing," said Jackie, leaning back in his chair. "I'm actually glad it happened."

"...Why?"

Before Jackie could answer, Erin started talking. "So, Logan, I'm pretty sure you've heard by now? You know, that I'm planning to ask you to be my date to the Town Fair and all?"

"Oh. Yeah, I guess I have heard that. People say lots of things all the time, though."

"Well... do you want to go with me?"

"Oh. Well... I dunno, Erin. Do people really bring dates to the *fair* anymore?"

"Sure they do!"

"Excuse me, ladies and gentlemen. Are we going to have social hour all day, or are we ready to begin?" boomed the voice of Mr. Leland Kowalski, a bespectacled man with an affinity for argyle.

"I'm *so* ready!" answered Jackie, slapping his desk in excitement.

At lunch that day, Jackie and Logan sat across from one another in the cafeteria, Logan munching on a bag of potato chips and Jackie guzzling down a Mountain Dew.

"I don't get it, though," said Logan. "Will they even let a boy sign up for the pageant?"

"No. I'm pretty sure it's against the rules. That's why they're not gonna know."

"What do you mean, they're not gonna *know*?"

"I mean... Jackie Almond. It's not like it's never confused anyone before."

"So you're gonna lie?" Logan asked through a mouthful of chips.

"No, dude. How is that lying? It's my *name*. It's their fault if they assume things."

"I don't know. Something just doesn't seem right about it."

"What's the matter? You have a problem with guys being pretty too?" Jackie asked, smiling.

"Oh shut *up*, Jackie!" said Logan, throwing his bag of chips at Jackie's face.

In a classroom down the hall, Steph and Erin sat with a few other girls on top of a group of desks arranged in a circle. "Feminist Club Meeting" was written in big, loopy letters on the chalkboard. The girls ate their lunches as they talked.

"So, what's the first order of business today?" asked a muscular girl sitting to Steph's right.

"Oh, I've got something," said Steph, chewing a mouthful of mac n' cheese. Next to her butt sat a bag of M&Ms and a pack of mini-donuts from the vending machine. The Ziploc bag of celery that Debra had stealthily slipped into her lunch bag had found its rightful home in the trash can. "Are y'all going to the fair this weekend?"

The girls nodded, most of them murmuring affirmative responses about there being nothing better to do this weekend anyway.

"Well, the Fair Queen pageant is this Saturday. Or, at least... it's *supposed* to be," said Steph. Her heart fluttered a little with excitement as she prepared to reveal the idea she'd been planning ever since she walked away from Debra's phone conversation the night before.

"*Supposed* to be?" asked Erin.

"Right," said Steph. "Every year the fair hosts an event that judges the women of Grey Acres the same way it judges its vegetables and livestock. So we're going to destroy it."

"We're going to *destroy* you." Lizzie Simon stood at the front of her third-grade classroom, holding up a picture of a pumpkin with a blue ribbon on it. *What does the fair mean to you?* the chalkboard behind her asked. Her teacher, the droopy-eyed Mary Ann Pegsworth, sat hunched over at her desk, resting her head in one hand and half-listening to the students' presentations.

"We destroy everyone every year," Lizzie continued. "Simon family pumpkins are *incomparable.*"

"Nice use of vocab words, Lizzie," said Mrs. Pegsworth.

Terry Almond sat at his desk with starry eyes and a dumb grin on his face. "Sí. Muy bien, señorita."

"Ugh. What does that even *mean*?" asked Lizzie.

Terry shrugged, smiling and raising his eyebrows at her.

"You know what? It doesn't *matter* what it means. Because I'm gonna kick your butt in the pumpkin growing contest, Terry. The Simons are *champions of cultivation!*"

Without looking up from her desk, Mrs. Pegsworth halfheartedly applauded Lizzie. "Nice job. Way to use the vocab words. Gold star. Who's next?"

Lizzie walked back to her desk and sat down.

"You're *on*," said Terry.

After school that afternoon, Jackie and Logan walked around the run-down lobby of the Grey Acres Mall. They went through the food court—which contained only three tables, a small Crunchy's Chicken kiosk, and an Asian smoothie place called "Asian Smoothies"—and into the main part of the mall, which featured a nail salon with no customers, a pet store that sold mostly reptiles, an arcade that closed twenty-three years ago, and Feinstein's Department Store, which Logan's dad owned. Jackie and Logan headed toward Feinstein's, passing a few benches surrounding a large fountain that had been turned off for at least a few years or so.

"Hey, remember when we took Nora and Laura on that double date here? When we were in, like, eighth grade?" said Jackie.

"Yeah, I remember. They kept trying to be all romantic. Like, 'Let's throw coins in the fountain together and make wishes!'"

"Yeah, and I had to be like, 'Hell no, ladies, all I have is quarters and I need those for the laundromat. And in case you haven't noticed, there is no water in the fountain.'"

Logan laughed. He tried to remember his days as a womanizer as fondly as he could, or at least have a little sense of humor about the situation.

"They were so disappointed, too," said Jackie, shaking his head, as they approached Feinstein's Department Store. "So, your dad can get me a discount here, right?" Jackie asked as the boys pushed open the double doors together.

"Yup. Except on red-sticker sale items. Those prices are final."

Feinstien's Department Store was a nice contrast from the rest of the mall, with its clean floors and large selections of clothes, perfume, and jewelry. Jackie and Logan passed the menswear section, full of blazers, ties, and folded dress shirts, then trekked through the horrible perfume department, plugging their noses as middle-aged women sprayed perfume samples all around them.

"Okay, but I don't have to actually *show* your dad what I'm buying, right?" Jackie asked, his voice nasal from his fingers holding his nose.

"Right," said Logan's equally nasal voice. "I'll just show my license to the cashier and we should be good. Why?"

Jackie and Logan let go of their noses as they entered the Juniors' Section, aimed at teen girls. The walls were decorated with posters of teenage girls modeling the store's clothes outside in a pretty fall environment that was definitely not Grey Acres. Neon-pink light-up letters hung on the wall, spelling out PROM. Under the letters were racks and racks of tacky dresses made of tulle and fake silk, some covered in sequins, all in various shades of obnoxious colors.

"Now that's just shitty advertising," said Logan, pointing to the prom sign. "Prom isn't even for seven months. I'll have to talk to my dad about that."

Jackie didn't answer. He was too busy staring at the racks in front of him, scanning the options. "Do you think I'd look good in pink?" asked Jackie.

"Not really. You hair color would work better with either a medium blue, or maybe like a dark purple. Wait, *why*?"

Jackie rifled through the dresses on hangers, quickly darting from rack to rack as Logan followed behind, a worried expression on his face as Jackie's plan started coming together in his mind.

"Shit. I don't think girls' sizes work like guys' do," said Jackie. "How can you be a zero? Wouldn't that imply that there's nothing there? Like no circumference or volume or anything?"

"I don't know. I guess you could ask a sales associate for help. Feinstein's sales associates are smart, skilled, and eager to help."

"You should come up with a better motto," said Jackie, keeping his eyes on the dresses in front of him. "The third part needs to start with an S too. Like maybe, 'smart, skilled, and seeking to help,' or something. I dunno. You're the English guy. Make some parallelism happen."

"It's already parallel," said Logan. "Do you mean alliteration?"

"Whatever, dude," replied Jackie, too focused on the formalwear in front of him to care for an English lesson from Logan. He pushed a metallic-gold sequined ball gown to the side and looked at a floor-length teal halter dress. Shaking his head slightly, he pushed that one aside as well.

Logan rolled his eyes as he watched Jackie's expression turn from one of eagerness to one of pained confusion. "Do you want me to find someone to help you?"

Jackie shook his head. "Nah. I'm gonna eyeball it." He grabbed a random cluster of hangers off the rack.

A few minutes later, Logan sat on a bench outside the fitting room, twiddling his thumbs as he waited for Jackie inside. On the ground next to him, he spotted a discarded newspaper with the front-page headline, "Pageant Predictions: Who Will Be This Year's Face of Grey Acres?" Underneath the headline were amateur headshots of previous years' pageant winners. Logan picked up the newspaper and started reading.

The majority of the article turned out to be an interview with last year's Fair Queen, Becky Norman, and her thoughts on what the title meant. "To me, being Fair Queen shows Grey Acres that our town's greatest accomplishment isn't our top-notch school system," (a lie) "our thriving economy," (a much bigger lie) "or our award-winning agriculture;" (true, even if most of those awards were won within the town itself) "it's our *people*." Logan chuckled at the grandiosity of Becky's statement, and pictured Jackie trying to say something like that on stage with a straight face. The next question asked Becky what she thought were the most important qualities of a Fair Queen. "Easy! A can-do attitude, a love for the beautiful town of Grey Acres, and, of course, an in-your-face shade of lipstick!" Logan cringed so hard his face contorted a little. He'd had a few English classes with Becky Norman over the years. Every essay she shared with the class managed to contain at least three try-hard jokes that totally fell flat. That was Becky's style, though. Making masses of people groan, and wearing in-your-face shades of lipstick.

Logan's reading was suddenly halted when Jackie flung open the door to the fitting room. He looked up at Jackie, standing in the doorway wearing a tight dark purple dress that stopped at least half a foot above his knees. It was covered in silver sequins and had a bright yellow rose attached to the left sleeve.

"Dark purple works for me, right?" Jackie asked.

Logan burst out laughing. "Oh, God. I think Melanie Catsman wore that exact dress when I took her to the eighth-grade Valentine's dance."

"It's forty dollars now, so with your dad's discount, what would that be?"

"Come on, Jackie. You're not *really* gonna do this."

"I am. It's better than asking my mom if I can borrow one of her evening gowns."

"What Heather Almond thinks passes for an evening gown is scarily inaccurate. But seriously, Jackie. You have no idea what kind of crazy stuff you're gonna start."

At that moment, a sixty-something-year-old fitting room attendant, wearing grandma glasses and carrying a stack of unwanted clothes, entered the fitting room area.

"What are you doing?" she asked Jackie.

"Oh, I'm glad you're here. Is this how it's supposed to fit, or do you think I should go a size up?"

The attendant stared at Jackie, a blank expression on her face.

"Sorry, it's just that I don't know how girl sizes work."

"That's because you're a boy," she said.

"Yes, I know that," said Jackie. "Hence my trouble with the girl sizes. So, could you help me out?"

"Please leave the girls' fitting room area," said the attendant.

"Okay. I can do that. But do you think if I brought some of these over to the men's fitting room they could help me there?" Jackie gestured toward a slew of tacky dresses he had hanging on hooks in the fitting room stall.

"That's it. I want you two hooligans out of my store."

"You can't throw us out," said Jackie.

"I absolutely can," said the attendant.

"And it's not *your* store. It's *his* store, actually." Jackie pointed to Logan, who was still sitting on the bench reading the newspaper. Logan looked up at Jackie and started vigorously shaking his head no, but Jackie, still facing the attendant, did not notice.

"What do you mean it's 'his' store?" asked the attendant.

"I'll have you know that my buddy Logan here's dad is *the* Mr. Feinstein."

Logan leapt up from the bench and grabbed Jackie's arm. He started walking, pulling Jackie out of the fitting room area with him.

Logan dragged Jackie through the girls' clothing section as they headed back toward the door.

"What'd I do?" Jackie asked.

"Oh, come on. You should *know* not to bring my dad into this!"

Logan continued to pull Jackie through the horrible perfume department and back through the menswear near the entrance. As they reached the door and Logan tried to pull Jackie out of the store, the alarm sounded with a blaring wail. They stopped. Store patrons all around them stared.

Logan looked at Jackie. He was still wearing the dress.

Chapter Four
Wednesday

The sun hadn't fully risen yet, leaving the sky a mix of greyish-blue and pinkish-orange. Debra and Lizzie were on their knees in the middle of Simon's Pumpkin Farm, watering and applying liquid fertilizer to various growing pumpkins.

Lizzie sang as she worked. "If you need a pumpkin, we're better than the rest. Simon family pumpkins are the *best, best, best!*"

Debra glanced at her watch. "It's after 6:30," she said. "Can you go drag Stephanie out of bed? I told her last night we'd need her help."

"Oh. She left a note on the fridge saying she had to go to school early this morning for Mathletes practice. Maybe she'll help in the afternoon."

Debra sighed. "That girl's gonna put me in an early grave, I'm telling you."

Lizzie ignored Debra's complaint and continued to sing while she watered a pumpkin. "We've got the best pumpkins in the nation. The Simons are champions of cultivation!"

Meanwhile, in the high school library, Steph sat at a computer, her fingers flying across the keys. She finished typing, clicked the print button, and sat back in her chair, smiling as she admired her work. The printer violently spit out pages upon pages.

Steph paced around the school lobby with a clipboard, waiting for students to arrive. Slowly, exhausted-looking students with droopy eyes filed into the building. Steph approached a boy wearing pajama pants and a sweatshirt and slowly sipping coffee (which, from the smell of it, seemed to be a maple-syrup-flavored latte from Paul's Pancake World) from a travel mug. She pushed the clipboard toward his face. "Want to sign a petition to end the pageant and the misogyny that goes along with it?" She held up a flyer that said, "The Pageant is Un-'Fair'. Come to Room 206 After School for More Information!"

He yawned. "What?"

"Every year, the Grey Acres Town Fair takes part in the tradition of teaching young women that they should be valued solely for their appearance—"

"If I sign, will you not talk at me so loud?"

Steph nodded and handed him the clipboard and a pen. He signed. She grabbed it back from him and ran after Katie Thomas, a thin, fairly attractive girl she recognized from a few of her classes. "Hey, Katie! Want to sign a petition to end the Fair Queen pageant and its inherent misogyny?"

"You're kidding, right?" Katie pushed past Steph and walked down the hallway to class. As she walked away, Steph noticed a hot pink ribbon safety-pinned to Katie's backpack, which read, "93rd Grey Acres Fair Queen Runner-Up."

Meanwhile, Jackie, wearing a thick sweater and a baseball cap, stood at his locker, searching for his textbook and notebook for his first-period history class. As he rifled through old papers and a few used tissues and candy wrappers, he felt the cap being swept off his head. He turned around to see Flounder standing next to him, now holding his cap.

"No hats in school, Mr. Almond," said Flounder. "It's disrespectful."

"Forgive me, Mr. Flounder, but class hasn't even started yet."

"Doesn't matter. You're in the building. It's disrespectful. I currently feel disrespected."

Jackie rolled his eyes and turned back to his locker.

"Don't you roll your eyes at me, Jackson."

"Jackie."

Flounder handed Jackie's cap back to him. "And don't spend all weekend canoodling and shenanigan-ing at the fair. You *will* have the first draft of your college essay to me by Monday morning, I presume?"

Jackie turned his head to face Flounder. "Damn *right* I will."

Flounder raised an open fist to his mouth and pantomimed thrusting an object in and out.

Jackie made a face. He was at least 70 percent sure that Flounder had no idea what his gesture looked like. "What are you *doing*?"

"I'm washing my mouth out with soap. As a reminder for *you* to watch your language." Flounder began to back away from Jackie, still facing him the entire time. "Now go to class. Keep your hat off. Write your essay!" Flounder turned around and walked away.

Jackie turned back to his locker and continued searching for books, but this time was distracted by Logan tapping his shoulder. Jackie turned his head.

"My dad thinks you're gay," said Logan.

"So? My dad thinks you're gay, too."

"That's different," Logan explained. "Jack Sr.'s just perceptive. My dad was more like, 'Tell your gay friend not to try stealing any more prom dresses from my store.'"

"Did you tell him they're not really prom dresses since it's October?"

Logan rolled his eyes. "Look, don't bring my dad into this anymore, okay? You know that my parents don't know yet."

"They don't know that prom's in the spring? I thought everyone knew that. *Especially* people running a department store that sells prom dresses."

"Jackie, I'm serious! Can you stop joking around for *one second* and just listen?"

Jackie froze, not expecting Logan's outburst. "Yeah. Um... sure. I'm sorry, man." He looked to

Logan, who still looked pissed. Jackie stuck his head back into his locker and rifled around for a moment until he found a bag of M&Ms. He pulled them out of the locker and held them out to Logan, a peace offering. "Buddy?"

Logan ripped the bag open and threw an M&M in his mouth. "Okay. But I'm serious. No more run-ins with Papa Feinstein."

The bell rang. Jackie closed his locker and walked down the hallway with Logan. "Don't worry, bud," said Jackie. "I've decided not to do the whole cross-dressing thing anyway. I think I should win on my own style, you know? Get myself a well-fitting suit. Show Grey Acres that being the Fair Queen is *truly about being yourself.*"

"You have a lot more faith in Grey Acres than I do."

Jackie had at least enough faith in Grey Acres to spend his lunch period sitting at a computer in the library, attempting to sign up as an official pageant contestant. He opened Internet Explorer (the only official browser supported by Grey Acres High School) and went to greyacrestownfair.com, a website that was constructed sometime after the school first got Internet in 2002 and had been updated zero times. He clicked on a pink rectangular button with purple Comic Sans text inside, reading "Fair Queen Pageant Signup (Girls Ages 14-18 Only)." The computer's arrow turned to an hourglass and Jackie sat waiting for a moment, impatiently drumming his fingers on the desk. He shoved some potato chips in his mouth while he waited, making a loud *crunch* as he chewed.

"*Shhhh!*" snapped Janice Hooper, the eighty-five-year-old librarian sitting behind the circulation desk. Everyone always joked about how Mrs. Hooper would've retired twenty years ago if anyone in Grey Acres ever made enough money to retire. Well, it was probably more a depressing truth than a joke, but at least it earned her the cool nickname "the Octogenarian Librarian" from a few students. "No food in the library," she added, the wrinkly skin on her face jiggling a little with every syllable she uttered.

Finally, a form appeared on the website. Jackie had no trouble typing in his basic information—name, date of birth, etc.—but froze up when the questions became a bit more specialized. For one thing, he wasn't sure what to put in the required text box asking about his three favorite places in

Grey Acres. If he were being honest, his *only* favorite place was Almond's Convenience Store, since it was owned by his dad and provided him with money. But he was worried that if he put that, whoever was reading the form would focus more on the "Almond" part than the "Jackie" part, and if that person turned out to be someone who frequented the convenience store, they may have remembered a kid named Jackie making their sandwich and working the cash register and being a male. He was also reluctant to put Feinstein's Department Store, in case word of finding a boy trying to sneak out in a prom dress had spread at all. So now everything was difficult, because Jackie was realizing there weren't all that many other places in Grey Acres to choose from. He ended up answering with Gus's Supermarket, Crunchy's Chicken, and Grey Acres High School, figuring the answers were generic enough not to arouse suspicion.

The other open-ended question, "What is your talent?" also slowed him down for a moment. He briefly considered writing "my dick," but laughed the idea away. Instead, he wrote, "It's a surprise :)."

He smiled and chuckled to himself a little. The smiley face was a nice touch.

Feeling decently confident in his answers, Jackie clicked the submit button. He then spent the rest of the lunch period watching the frozen hourglass on the computer screen and trying to eat potato chips silently, which involved thoroughly sucking the salty crunch out of each chip before descending his teeth upon a soft slice of mush.

Upon hearing the bell ring, Jackie stood up to leave the library, loudly crumpling his empty potato-chip bag in his hand and earning himself an extra glare from Mrs. Hooper. He threw the balled-up chip bag into the library trash can and would have walked away like usual, had it not been for the paper he found sitting on top of the rest of the garbage. Checking to make sure Mrs. Hooper wasn't looking in his direction, Jackie pulled Steph's flyer out of the trash can. He then made his way out of the library, reading the flyer as he walked, and scrunching his eyebrows as he read.

After school that day, Jackie followed Steph's poster to room 206. When he entered, Steph was already sitting on the teacher's desk, confidently swinging her legs and watching the group of ten or so students bustling in front of her as they looked for desks. Erin was the only person Jackie recognized.

"Steph, what's going on here?" Jackie asked.

"We're having a discussion on why the pageant is un-'fair'. You like my pun?"

"What?" Jackie looked at Steph, but she had already turned her attention back to the crowd of students in front of her.

"Order!" she shouted.

The students quieted down and found desks. Jackie quickly took a seat at the first desk he found.

"Thank you all for coming," Steph continued. "As I'm *sure* you all know, since *no one* in this goddamn town will shut up about it, the annual Town Fair is coming to us this Saturday. But I'm tired of going to a fair every year that fosters the notion that women should be awarded for their looks, the same way that plants and vegetables are. We're people, not pumpkins. That's why this year, I propose that we *end* the pageant. I've already started a petition that I'll be turning into Mayor Peach this week, which all of you should sign at the end of this meeting. But I also thought we should come up with some other ideas to sabotage the pageant should the petition fail—"

"You can't do that!" Jackie shouted, leaping up so quickly he almost knocked his desk over.

Steph, a little taken aback, looked at Jackie. "What? Is there a problem?"

Jackie glanced around the room, suddenly realizing that not only were all eyes on him, but that he hadn't prepared a rebuttal. "Yeah... um... you can't get rid of the pageant."

"Why not?"

"Because... uh... I like it."

"You *like* it?"

Jackie nodded. Despite the growing whispers of students around them, Steph never broke eye contact.

"You're telling me that you *support* this fair judging *women* the same way it does *plants and livestock*?"

"No, not necessarily..." Jackie glanced around the room for support, but instead found ten sets of eyes eagerly watching him and Steph.

"Then why do you like it?"

"Because... it's fun?" He frantically searched his brain for something more substantial to say, until he started to feel a headache coming on and gave up.

All the while, Steph stared at him, completely expressionless. After a few moments of awkward silence, she spoke up. "Oh, I get it. You like looking at all the girls. Judging your future *prospects*. Is that how you and Logan decide on the next pair of girls you'll take to the dance or the mall or whatever?"

"No! It's not like that!"

"Then why do you like the pageant?"

Jackie stood still, staring at Steph. It was either reveal that he was entering the pageant as a boy and risk being disqualified, or stay silent and let Steph's plans come to fruition. *Maybe there's a loophole*, Jackie thought, *some clever way out of this?* But in the moment, no words came.

"Well, whatever it is you *like* about the pageant," said Steph, "*don't* expect it to be here come this Saturday."

That night, Logan sat on the roof of the convenience store with a ten-pound hardcover Shakespeare anthology, reading *Hamlet* with a flashlight while he waited for Jackie. Once he heard the familiar footsteps coming up the ladder, he closed the book with a *thud*, watching a few snowflakes of dust fly out from between the pages.

"Hey, buddy. Sorry I'm late. Annoying old ladies at the deli wouldn't shut up again."

"I thought the deli closed at nine though?"

"Yeah. So did I." Jackie sat down next to Logan and glanced at the hefty book in his lap. "I see you've graduated from newspapers?"

"The newspapers here are depressing as hell," said Logan.

"Oh, right. I forgot that Shakespeare always writes about butterflies, sunshine, and stable job markets."

"It's different, man. Shakespeare is *profoundly depressing*."

"Whatever, dude."

"*Anyway*," said Logan, "you said we had an emergency to deal with tonight?"

"Yeah, okay, long story short, Steph's assembled this crazy-ass mob to sabotage the pageant."

"Why?"

"I don't know, because of feminism and stuff, I guess."

"Yeah, but you're entering it as a *guy*. Shouldn't that *help* her cause?"

"I mean, *theoretically*, yes, but nobody can *know* I'm entering as a guy. I'll get disqualified. Plus, she's already got this petition that like ten billion people are gonna sign that she's planning to give to the mayor, and she's got all these people helping her come up with these crazy ideas..."

"Okay," said Logan, nodding as he processed Jackie's problem. "Well, what are you gonna do?"

"I mean, I guess I'm gonna have to sabotage her back."

"How?"

"Okay, well," Jackie started, bracing himself for the reaction he knew Logan would have to his plan, "here's what I was thinking. So Erin is Steph's best friend, right? And she's helping Steph with this whole operation. And Erin seems to like *you* a lot. So..."

"Oh God, Jackie, I do not like where this is going..."

"Dude, it's gonna be easy. Just take Erin on, like one or two dates, see what you can find out about Steph's plans, and report back to me. That's all. It's not like I'm asking you to marry the girl."

"No. No, no, no, no, *no*. I don't do that kind of thing anymore, and you *know* that."

Jackie sighed, his shoulders falling as he pondered the situation. "Yeah, you're right, man. I'm sorry. The whole idea was stupid. I'll think of something else."

Jackie spent the rest of the night on his living room couch, staring at the ceiling and desperately trying to think of new ideas. On the TV, a Spanish soap opera played. Dramatic piano music served as the background to a bunch of fast-talking characters violently yelling at each other in Spanish.

Terry sat cross-legged in front of the TV, enjoying the soap opera, a small ceramic pot filled with dirt sitting in his lap. He picked up a pack of pumpkin seeds on the floor next to him and ripped it open. Then, he gently placed each seed in the pot and covered it with dirt. He stood up and walked to the windowsill, where he had left a floral-print paper cup of water. He slowly poured the water onto the seeds, then took a Sharpie out of his pocket and drew a big smiley face on the pot. As he began to lovingly pat the soil, he heard Jackie let out a loud sigh.

"What's wrong, hermano?" asked Terry.

"Just stupid fair stuff," grumbled Jackie.

"The fair isn't stupid. It's *wonderful!*" Terry exclaimed, spinning in circles around the room with his potted plant.

"It *might* be wonderful if stupid Stephanie Simon weren't out to ruin it for me."

Terry stopped spinning. He sat down on the couch, right on top of Jackie's legs. "Stephanie Simon? Is that Lizzie Simon's older sister?"

"I think so. Why?"

"Because *I'm* gonna beat Lizzie Simon in the vegetable contest this year! That girl is going *down!*"

Jackie laughed a little at his brother. "That whole family's out to get us, I guess."

"Two families at war! How romantic!" Terry stood up and waltzed around the living room with his potted plant. A romantic string quartet began playing on the TV as the characters shouted "¡Te quiero!" and "¡Mi amor!" at one another. Terry, looking up at the ceiling, dreamily pranced around in circles.

Jackie bolted upright. "Yo, Terry, you wanna help me out?"

Meanwhile, Logan sat awkwardly slouched in a velvet armchair in his living room. He glanced around the room at the plants in elaborate vases and framed still-lifes hanging on the walls, doing anything to keep his gaze from hitting Ronald and Sheila Feinstein, who sat side-by-side on the couch across from him. Ronald still had his tie on and his shirt fully buttoned. They both held teacups in one hand and saucers in the other, periodically taking small sips of tea.

"We're just *concerned*, honey," said Sheila.

Logan rolled his eyes.

"What kind of name is *Jackie* for a young man, anyway?" asked Ronald.

Logan shrugged. "I think there was a girl named Logan on my baseball team in, like, second grade."

Ronald looked at Sheila and shook his head. "Co-ed sports. That's where this shit starts."

Sheila nodded knowingly and took a small sip of tea before looking back to Logan. "Look, sweetie, we don't mean to pry. It just seems like you and Jackie spend an *awful* lot of time together—"

"Up on that convenience store roof doing *God-knows-what*—" Ronald interjected.

"And we just wanted to make sure that..."

"I mean, the boy was in my store wearing a *prom* dress for God's sake!"

Logan furrowed his eyebrows in disgust, almost gagging a little. "Oh God, no. Jackie and I are best *friends*, okay? Jackie's not even *like* that."

"And *you*?" asked Ronald.

"And I..." Logan watched Sheila and Ronald sip their tea in unison. His eyes darted back and forth between them. They simultaneously set their saucers on the coffee table, set their cups on the saucers, folded their hands in their laps, and stared at Logan. "*I*... have a date with a girl tomorrow night."

"Oh honey," said Sheila, smiling and dramatically touching her hand to her heart. "That's *wonderful*! What's the lucky lady's name?"

"...Erin."

Ronald scoffed. "What kinda name's that for a girl?"

Chapter Five

Thursday

Thursday morning, the Grey Acres High School Mathletes were hosting their third-biggest rival team, the Fightin' Badgers of Blue Forest Academy. Steph always thought Blue Forest was a stupid name for a school, and an even stupider name for a town. The neighboring town of Blue Forest had a couple thousand beige suburban houses in it, and exactly zero forests. And besides, forests weren't blue. Sometimes flowers could be blue, but for the most part, blue was not a color associated with plant life of any kind. Despite the million and a half things Steph hated about Grey Acres, she at least appreciated that the town's name made sense. After all, the majority of the town was made up of acres, and the town did always feel very grey, at least emotionally. The one thing that the Blue Forest team did have going for them, Steph thought, was that they had a mascot. The Fightin' Badger was pretty cute in its blue turtleneck sweater, even if the school never brought its mascot along to Mathletes matches. Steph was at least a little jealous, since Grey Acres High never bothered to have a mascot, despite Debra's many offers over the past decade to sew some kind of pumpkin mascot costume.

In the final round of the Mathletes competition, Steph sat with the rest of the team in folding chairs on the stage in their high school auditorium. Wearing a royal blue long-sleeve button-down shirt and a houndstooth-patterned sweater vest, Steph sat second from the left, like she always did. Brad Thompson sat on the far left because he was still the team captain, despite Steph's eighth-grade attempt to get him banned from all future academic teams on the grounds of sexually harassing Erin. But the middle-school guidance counselor, Ms. Lobsman, was too drunk to care when Steph brought this issue up to her, so Brad stayed team captain all through high school, much to Steph's dismay.

As the second and final round of the competition neared its end, Steph tried to look out into the audience to see if Debra made it. Steph had mentioned the competition to her mom a few times, and Debra had said, "We'll see," which was more than she normally did, so Steph took that with at least a little optimism. But Steph was unable to see anything when she looked into the crowd, due to the stage lights blinding her. She blinked, trying to ignore the lights, as Mrs. Hooper, slow voice shaking, read the final question, which asked them to find the area of an irregular shape using an integral.

Steph scratched a few quick notes on the notepad on her lap before her thumb slammed down the red button on the buzzer in her hand. "Four hundred twenty-five," said Steph.

"Riiiight... yoooou... aaaare," Mrs. Hooper said, stretching those words out over nearly ten seconds. "And with that, the winner of today's match is Grey Acres High School. Congratulations, kids."

Steph, Brad, and their other two teammates, a pair of uptight, preppy twins named Leo and Theo, leapt up from their chairs and high-fived one another. Steph walked to the front of the stage to get a better look out into the audience. She scanned each row of chairs at least three times before concluding that Debra was not there. In the front row, though, she did see Lizzie, on her lunch break from the elementary school across the street, wearing a giant smile on her face and holding a laminated hall pass. Once she made eye contact with Steph, she gave her a big thumbs-up. Steph smiled at Lizzie, then gave her a thumbs-up back.

Later that afternoon, after school was over, Terry wandered into Simon's Pumpkin Farm holding a folded piece of yellow legal pad paper in his hand. Terry, wanting to keep his plans a secret between himself and Jackie, had told his mom that he was going to his new friend Eduardo's house. Eduardo's mom didn't speak English, and Heather Almond didn't speak Spanish, so the plan was pretty much foolproof.

Terry walked around the farm, studying each pumpkin he passed. He finally took a seat on one of the largest pumpkins, opened up his note, and read over his own jagged, messy handwriting.

Lizzie,

If you want your pumpken back, you'll meet me on the conveenyanse store roof with all the deetales of Steffaneys evil plan.

Love,

The Pumpkin Theef

Terry sighed as he folded his note back up. "Ay, caramba. El amor es una guerra," he said under his breath.

"Hello?" a familiar little girl's voice called.

Terry turned his head toward the Simon house to see Lizzie peeking her head out the back door. They locked eyes. Terry glanced from Lizzie to his note, then to the big pumpkin he was sitting on, then back to Lizzie, who had now walked out of the house and was heading towards him.

"¡Dios mío!" Terry shouted. He quickly started folding his yellow note into a paper airplane, though the nervous shaking of his fingers slowed him down a bit. He looked back up at Lizzie, whose pace toward him was quickening. He threw the paper airplane toward her. It sailed in the air for about six inches, then hit the ground.

Terry leapt up off of the pumpkin, crouched down, and wrapped his arms around it. He struggled with all the strength in his little eight-year-old arms to yank the pumpkin out of the ground, but the pumpkin wouldn't budge. He looked up at Lizzie, who was getting closer to him by the second. Terry quickly spotted a smaller pumpkin a few feet away and leapt toward it in one long stride. He glanced over his shoulder, saw Lizzie quickly approaching, and ripped the pumpkin out of the ground as fast as he could. Then, he ran.

Lizzie, stopping only to pick the paper airplane up off the ground, ran after him. She unfolded the airplane and read the note, the words bobbing up and down in front of her as she ran.

Terry, with his arms firmly clasping the pumpkin to his chest, quickly glanced over his shoulder to see if Lizzie was catching up. She was. He saw Lizzie crumple the paper airplane into a little ball in her hand, wind up her arm, and throw the paper ball straight at him. It hit him squarely in the face, which slowed him down for a moment, before he faced forward again and continued running.

Just then, he felt a force of about seventy pounds or so slam him in the back. Lizzie, her hands grasping Terry's shoulders, tackled him to the ground. As Terry fell forward, the small pumpkin slipped from his hands and flew out in front of him. It landed on the ground with a *thwack.* Terry's body slammed onto the grass face-first.

Lizzie flipped Terry's body over so she was facing him, still tightly gripping his shoulders. She held him pinned to the ground like a wrestler as she moved her face toward his, so close their noses almost touched.

"Listen here, Almond," she seethed. "You *don't* mess with Simon family pumpkins."

That night at the Grey Acres Mall, Logan and Erin sat side-by-side on the edge of the waterless fountain. Logan held a red-checkered cardboard basket of Crunchy's Chicken's waffle fries in his lap, which he and Erin both ate from. Erin held an Asian Smoothie with two straws.

Around them, the mall was slightly busier than usual, mostly because the normally customerless nail salon, Nails by Noelle Northberger, was bustling with potential Fair Queens getting their nails ready for the big day.

Logan glanced at Erin, who was adorably dressed in a 60s-style plaid jumper and white knee socks. He swallowed his current waffle fry and laughed nervously. "Hey, I'm sorry I didn't take you somewhere better tonight, but—"

"There isn't really anywhere? Trust me, I *know*."

They both giggled softly and simultaneously stuffed another waffle fry in their mouths. They chewed for a moment in awkward silence.

"So, uh, Erin... Tell me about yourself?" Logan sensed a clear awkwardness in the date, which, although he was ashamed to admit it, he was thankful for. If the date went badly, Erin wouldn't expect any more out of him, yet he could still utilize the date for its purposes of misleading his parents and acquiring information for Jackie. Of course, he didn't want to *purposely* make the date go badly. Then he'd worry that Erin would figure out he was using her. Which he didn't want to do in the first place. Logan silently cursed Jackie for being so mischievous. And Ronald and Sheila Feinstein for being so nosy.

"Oh, sure thing. What do you want to know?"

"Hmm. Well, how did you get into feminism?"

"Hmm." Erin looked up toward the ceiling, chewing on another waffle fry as she thought of an answer. "I think... I think it may have been freshman year. That was the first time I read *The Awakening*, and realized Kate Chopin was a feminist literary genius. I mean, that was when I got into feminism *outside* of listening to Steph yell about things."

Logan laughed, a genuine one this time. "The *first* time you read *The Awakening*?"

"Yeah. I mean, you can't read a book that great only *once*."

Logan nodded. "Oh, I totally agree. I've read it at least twice since we had to read it for school. It was just so much more fun to read on my own than in class."

"Right?" Erin laughed. "Oh my God, remember how much our class discussion *sucked*?"

"How could I forget? Every other comment was just Becky Norman going on and on about how she could never understand a woman who'd want to leave a rich husband."

"I know, right? The whole time I was just sitting there with this *insane* headache, and in my head I just kept yelling—"

"*Shut up, Becky!*" they both yelled at once. Then, they both burst out laughing at the same time. Logan felt a powerful excitement about talking to Erin, which was unfortunately clouded by an even more powerful guilt.

Meanwhile, as the convenience store was reaching its last hour before closing, Jackie stood behind the ice cream counter. Every few seconds, he scooped some ice cream out of the cookie-dough bucket, then dropped the scoop back in. He had almost accomplished both thoroughly killing his boredom and building a three-row ice-cream-scoop pyramid when he finally heard some customers approaching the counter.

He looked up to see Katie Thomas, a girl in his grade, standing in front of the counter. She was with her little sister, who excitedly bounced and twitched at the thought of ice cream, and her dad, who held a bright green leash that led to a sandy-haired Cocker Spaniel. Jackie considered telling them that animals weren't technically allowed in the store, but anyone who said that kind of thing in Grey Acres always ended up sounding like a broken record.

"Hi!" the little girl shouted. Jackie wondered for a second if the little girl knew Terry, but, after looking at her face for a moment, realized she was probably much younger. Jackie was always terrible at guessing ages.

"Hey, there," Jackie replied to her, leaning over the counter a little. "What can I get for you, sweetie?"

"Uuuuummmm." The little girl giggled. "A *big* ice cream cone! *Three* scoops! Chocolate! Uuummmm... *miiiint* chocolate! ...Peeeeeeeanut butter!"

"Coming right up!" Jackie dipped his ice cream scoop in a bucket of water, preparing to actually use it for its intended purpose.

"Katie, what do *yooouu* want?" Jackie heard the little girl ask her older sister while he dropped the first scoop of ice cream onto the cone.

"Sweetie, you know your sister isn't eating ice cream until *after* the fair on Saturday," the dad said.

Jackie accidentally dropped the second scoop of ice cream back into the tub. He'd seen this before. And though this time there was no long line of customers to hold up, he had no interest in seeing it again.

"Aww, but Katie *loves* ice cream!" said the little girl.

Jackie silently glared at the dad as he handed a newly built ice cream cone across the counter to the little girl. "Here you go."

"Thank yooooouu!" she squealed, excitedly licking the drops of ice cream that were starting to melt around the cone's rim.

The dad rifled through his wallet. Jackie was about to tell him that he could take the ice cream and pay at the cash register on the other side of the store, but he stopped. He looked at Katie, whose eyes drooped a little in sadness. Was it sadness, Jackie wondered, or exhaustion due to food deprivation? He looked at the little girl eating ice cream, her grin growing with every lick. He looked at the dog staring at the ice cream, his drools giving the dripping ice cream a run for its money.

Looking back at the dad, Jackie finally spoke up. "Come on, man. Just buy Katie some freaking ice cream."

"Excuse me?" he asked.

"Jackie, don't—" Katie interjected.

"One ice cream cone isn't gonna kill her."

"Is that really how you talk to your customers?" asked the dad, stepping forward to bring his face closer to Jackie's. Unfortunately, along with his step forward, he ended up bumping into the little girl. It wasn't a hard enough bump to knock her to the floor, but it was hard enough to make her stumble, causing the ice cream cone to slip from her hands.

"*Aaaaaaeeeeeeeeehhhhhhhhh!*" The little girl let out one of the most piercing screams Jackie had ever heard. His eyes even watered a little. Without a second of hesitation, the dog began rapidly licking up all of the ice cream on the floor.

Trying his best to ignore the screams, Jackie exaggeratedly rolled his eyes at the dad. "Sorry, but I wasn't expecting a lesson in tact from a blatant misogynist." Jackie silently thanked Logan for teaching him those last two words.

"Seriously, where do you come off talking to your customers like that?" The dad was now raising his voice. "My daughter's eating habits are *none* of your business."

"Um, *all* of this is my business," said Jackie, shouting just loud enough to be heard over the child's yelling. "Because it's *my* store."

"No, it's *my* store," boomed a voice from behind him.

Jackie turned his head to see his father speed-walking out of the back room, making a beeline for the ice cream counter. "Now, sir..." Jack Sr. tried to get the dad's attention, but his voice was quickly drowned out as the little girl's shrieks turned into long-winded wails. To add to the noise, the dog started coughing. "Sir..." he tried again, but now the dog's coughs grew louder and louder, until the dog finally vomited ice cream all over the floor.

The dad grabbed his younger daughter's hand and dragged her and the dog out of the store, paying no mind to the vomit puddle in front of the ice cream counter. Katie followed behind, but not without first glancing back at Jackie, glaring and shaking her head.

As the family left and the noise died down, Jack Sr. took a moment to close his eyes and take a deep breath. After a few seconds of silence, he finally spoke. "Jackie, what did you think you were doing? *How* many times have I told you that you're not allowed to argue with the customers?"

"But didn't you see that guy, Dad? He was being an asshole!"

"Yeah. And *now* he's an asshole who never paid me for his ice cream." Jack Sr. shook his head and started walking toward the back room again. "Expect that ice cream cone to be deducted from your paycheck, Jackie," he called. He disappeared into the back room, as Jackie faintly heard him mumble, "I'm getting too old for this."

Most of the Grey Acres Mall stores closed well before ten, so Logan had decided to walk Erin home. As they walked past rows of spread-out one-story houses, Logan realized that he and Erin had barely stopped talking all evening.

"...So, to bring us back to what we *first* started talking about," said Erin, "that's why I think Kate Chopin is a legend."

"That's interesting," Logan replied. "I mean, I guess I've just always looked at her solely from a literary perspective, and never really considered the feminist implications."

"Well, the *next* time you read it—"

"Oh, you *know* there will be a next time—"

"Try looking at it from both perspectives."

Logan smiled. "I think I will."

They walked up Erin's short driveway and stopped next to her front door. The two of them stood there for a moment, just looking at one another.

"Well, I can confidently say that this was one of the best dates I've ever had."

"Me too, actually." Logan smiled, one-third genuinely, one-third nervously, one-third guiltily.

"I'm, uh... as nerdy as this sounds, I'm glad to finally find someone who wants to talk about books all night. I mean, Steph's great, but she's, you know, kind of a math person..."

"Yeah, and you know, Jackie's great, but he's just kind of a... just not a book person..."

"Yeah." Erin laughed a little. "Thanks for a great night, Logan."

Logan watched as Erin looked up at him, smiling. He felt a tension building inside of him, realizing that this was one of those moments where it seemed like they were about to kiss and would be weird if they didn't. His blood heated up a little and his brain started to ache as he tried to figure out what to do. Finally, he leaned forward, and he and Erin kissed.

Two seconds later, he forcefully pulled his face away.

"What's wrong?" Erin asked.

"It's just... why do you have to be so great?"

"What do you mean?"

"Why do you have to be, like, the perfect girl for me? *Why* am I an awful human being?"

"Soy un hombre malo. ¿Por *qué*?" Terry yelled, dramatically flopping backwards onto his living-room couch. Above his head, he held his smiley-face potted plant, which was still a pile of soil with no green sprouts to speak of. He stared into its Sharpie eyes.

Jackie stood in the doorway to the living room, leaning against the wall, cell phone in hand as he waited for a text update from Logan. "What's wrong, little bro?" Jackie asked.

Terry sat up on the couch and sadly petted the orange ceramic pot. "I tried to steal Lizzie's pumpkin. Now she's never gonna talk to me again."

"So?" asked Jackie, shrugging. "I thought you guys were enemies."

Terry shook his head. "No me gusta la guerra. Da a la gente el dolor."

"Dude. I have no idea what you're saying."

Terry didn't respond. Instead, he stared at his plant, lost in sadness.

"So," Jackie tried, "did you end up getting any information about Steph's plans?"

Terry shook his head, never breaking eye contact with the plant.

Logan hadn't expected a fight. He knew Jackie's plans were risky, and he knew he had to be careful, but he hadn't expected it all to blow up in his face so quickly. Logan was usually good with plans and strategizing. But there he stood, on Erin's doorstep, as her arms alternated between flailing wildly in angry gestures and being defiantly folded across her chest.

"I just don't get what *other motives* is supposed to mean," she said. "And I don't get why you won't explain it to me. I think you *at least* owe me that."

"Look, I'm sorry, okay? I told you, I'm a horrible person."

"Yeah," Erin scoffed. "I gathered that."

"This whole situation is *really* complicated, okay? And I'm just not sure you'll understand."

"I won't *understand*? Forgive me, but I thought I spent the whole *night* understanding you. All that business about me being the smartest girl you've ever taken out, and the first one you've really

87

connected with. Unless that was just part of your *other motives* bullshit, too."

"No, Erin, it's not like that. It's just..." He took a deep breath, trying to figure out what to say next, when Erin cut him off.

"It's Jackie, isn't it?"

"No! God, you sound like my dad. Look, Jackie and I are just *friends*—"

"What? I meant because of him and Steph. And that stupid war they're having."

"War?"

Erin rolled her eyes. "You know what I'm talking about. Steph said Jackie got his brother to steal her sister's pumpkin or something so she'd give up her plans. It's so stupid. I thought maybe Jackie roped you into this as well. Am I right?"

Logan stared at the ground. He noticed a few flower pots on Erin's doorstep, but for some reason, was more interested in studying the cracks in the cement between his feet. "I meant it when I said you were the perfect girl. So I'm gonna be totally honest with you right now, okay?"

"About time."

Logan looked up at Erin, with her eyes slightly squinted and her mouth twisted in a way that made

THE MAKING OF A SMALL-TOWN BEAUTY KING

it obvious she was trying to look angry. That way, he wouldn't notice the tears starting to form in her eyes. "Jackie initially wanted me to do that, yes. You got me. But I didn't want to use you like that. So I told him no. But then there was more to it."

"Like what?"

"Like... Okay, so I haven't been on a date with a girl in almost four years. And I was spending all my time with Jackie, right? And then a bunch of other weird shit happened and... my parents started thinking I was gay."

"Well?"

"Well what?"

"Are you?"

Logan made perfect eye contact with Erin, pausing for a moment before he slowly started nodding.

"Wow." Erin broke eye contact to look down at her shoes.

"Nobody except Jackie knows though, okay? And, well, now you too, I guess."

Erin nodded, saying nothing as she let herself process the information.

"So if it's all right, I'd appreciate if you'd keep it to yourself."

Erin suddenly lost all interest in her shoes and jolted her head upward, looking straight on at Logan. "And *what* motivation would I have to do that?"

"Excuse me?"

"You knew I liked you, Logan. And you used me. And I'm sorry if it's inconvenient for you, but I don't take too well to that."

"Erin, please, just... what do you want in return? I'll do anything."

"Okay. Then how about you do for me what you couldn't do for Jackie?"

Logan's eyes widened in disgust. He felt a rush of blood to his face. "Woah. Look, I told you, I'm *not* into—"

Erin rolled her eyes. "Ew. No, dummy. I mean, get his information. Report back to me on his plans. Help me and Steph destroy the pageant."

"Hold up here. A minute ago, you thought their fight was stupid. Now, you're being just as manipulative."

"Yup. Now you know how it feels." With that, Erin quickly turned away from Logan. She stepped into her house and slammed the door behind her, leaving Logan standing alone on the doorstep.

As the night drew to a close, Jackie and Terry sat side-by-side on the living room couch, the Spanish channel playing on the TV in front of them. Jackie slumped down in his seat, trying to invest himself in the lives of soap opera characters he couldn't understand, as he periodically checked his cell phone for an update from Logan. Terry continued to pet his plant. Suddenly, both boys were called to attention by the sound of their front door swinging open and banging shut.

Logan stormed through the Almonds' front hallway and entered the living room. "Jackie, this whole situation is fucked!"

Jackie gestured to Terry. "Watch your language, man." He even pantomimed Flounder's soap-thrusting movement, laughing.

"Don't worry, hermano. I'm good with languages," Terry interjected.

Logan firmly grabbed Jackie's wrist, stopping the weird soap-thrusting motion. "This isn't a *joke*, Jackie. You've got me in one messed up place right now."

"What'd I do?"

"There it is, Jackie. That *total* lack of self-awareness. It's like you don't even remember that you're the one who wanted to stir up all this trouble with the pageant. I *told* you, you had no idea what kinda shit you were gonna start."

Terry stood up from the couch, gently placed his plant back on the windowsill, and kissed it good night. He then walked out of the living room, waving to Jackie and Logan on his way out. "Buenas noches, amigos," he called.

Jackie stood up and waved as well. "Night, Terry." Then, he looked into Logan's eyes, which held an anger he'd never seen before. "What kinda shit did I start, Logan?"

"Are you kidding? You waged a war with Steph. *Steph*, Jackie. The loudest, most intense girl I *know*. Then, you gave me the *brilliant* idea of going on a date with Erin, who you *knew* liked me, just to manipulate her for information. And to top it all off, you had to go running around my dad's store in a prom dress, which made him have that weird talk with me, which *resulted* in me going on said date in the first place. I'd say you've screwed up pretty much everything."

"I don't get it. Did the date go badly or something?"

"What? You think a date where I intentionally lie to a girl and lead her on could possibly go *well*? I couldn't do it, Jackie. I told her the truth."

Jackie's eyes widened. "Why would you do that?"

"Because, as it turns out, if I did like girls, Erin would've been my perfect girlfriend. She was *amazing*, Jackie. I couldn't hurt her anymore. So now, of course, she's super pissed at me, and she knows everything, and she's gonna tell people I'm gay unless I switch sides and help her and Steph instead of you."

"What?!" Jackie started pacing back in forth in front of the couch, trying to process his best friend's impending betrayal. "You'd never do that to me, though, right?"

"Jackie. Have you been listening to *anything* I've been saying?"

Jackie stopped pacing and stood right in front of Logan. "Yeah, I have, man. And to be honest? I don't see what the big deal is. So this girl tells a few people you're gay. What's the worst thing that's gonna happen? Girls finally stop hitting on you?"

"No, the worst thing that could happen is that Ronald cuts me off from my friends. He already doesn't believe you and I are just friends as it is, and gives me a whole FBI-level interrogation every time I leave the house to go see you. Sheila falls into a crazy pit of depression because I'll never have a 'real Jewish wedding' or give her 'real Jewish grandchildren' like she's been talking about since I was a baby. This whole town stops taking me seriously and starts making fun of me like they do with, I dunno, Marvin Flounder or someone. Forgive me for making assumptions, but Grey Acres isn't known for being the most open-minded or progressive town out there."

"Exactly," said Jackie. "So why are you so afraid of making a statement? Saturday at the pageant, I'm going to be making a statement because I want this town to *change*. And I don't see why you can't get behind that."

"Honestly? I don't care what this town does. This town *sucks*. Right now, I'm just focusing on trying to get *out* of this town. And you seriously need to cut the bullshit with 'wanting the town to change' or whatever. You just want fancy colleges to pay attention to you."

"Yeah," Jackie rolled his eyes. "Because someone from Grey Acres going to a good college wouldn't be a welcome change *at all*, right? Look, I'm not some literary genius like you are. A lot of colleges wouldn't even *look* at me unless I did something big. So that's all I'm trying to do."

"Yeah? Well from now on, leave me out of it." With that, Logan pivoted around and stormed out of the room. Jackie saw him disappearing into the hallway, and finally heard the front door slam shut.

Just as Jackie was collapsing onto the couch, he heard footsteps coming down the stairs. Heather, dressed in a flannel bathrobe, poked her head into the living room doorway. Her eyes were half shut and had thick bags underneath them.

"Jackie, honey, it's a school night," she said. "Your father and I have to open the store at six tomorrow. So from now on, can you and Logan not have your teenage drama so late at night?"

Jackie nodded, muttered, "Sorry," and then fell onto his side on the couch. He watched his mother disappear back up the stairs as he slowly drifted off to sleep.

Chapter Six

Friday

Steph sat cross-legged on her bed, wide awake, as she watched the bright-green numbers on her alarm clock turn from 11:59 to 12:00. It was officially Friday, one day until the fair. She looked down at the petition lying in her lap, with only 23 of the 100 signature spots filled in. Other than Erin, all the students from her meeting on Wednesday had been largely unresponsive to her emails and texts. With a loud sigh, she flopped onto her back.

Though she tried to sleep, Steph ended up spending most of the night staring at her ceiling, anxious about thinking of a new plan fast enough to replace her failed petition. After almost an hour of restlessness had passed, Steph sat back up, turned on the lamp on her night stand, and committed herself to devising a new plan.

First, she spent a long time absentmindedly staring at her walls, which were painted a pale shade of pink. Debra had painted the walls pink as soon as Dr.-ish Fran Wellington, Grey Acres's only sort-of gynecologist, told her that her first child would be a girl. Steph didn't mind the walls for most of her life, since the color of the walls in her bedroom meant almost nothing in the grand scheme of things, and she didn't really hate the color that much anyway, even if it was sort of a boring color. But after starting high school, she asked Debra if they could paint her walls dark red instead.

"It's the color of MIT," Steph had told her mother.

"You're a freshman. What if you change your mind about where you want to go?" Debra had responded.

"Well, I still like the color either way."

"I'll be honest with you, honey. It's a little *intense*, don't you think?"

"Well, yeah, but that's fitting, isn't it? I mean, *I'm* a little intense."

Steph remembered Debra's slow nod, with her furrowed eyebrows, sympathetic eyes, and pursed lips. "Yeah, a little. You might want to work on that, sweetie."

So Steph's walls remained pale pink.

Steph looked at the shelf next to her dresser, which was lined with plaques and trophies from her four years on the Mathletes and three years on the Academic Team. Next to one of the plaques sat a framed picture of Steph, Lizzie, and Debra from last year's fair. They all stood around their award-winning pumpkin, which was almost as tall as Lizzie, and probably round enough to fit the three of them inside. The pumpkin wore a long blue sash which read "Best in Show" draped diagonally across it, similar to the way Debra was wearing hers in her 1989 Fair Queen photo. Too similar.

That's when it hit her. With ideas for a new plan rushing through her brain, Steph leapt out of bed, grabbed her Mathletes sweatshirt off the back of her desk chair, and pulled it over her head as she walked to the door. Then, so as not to wake up Debra or Lizzie, she quietly tiptoed down the stairs and toward the garage.

Five and a half hours later, the sun now fully up, Debra and Lizzie were on their knees in the middle of the pumpkin patch, harvesting pumpkins for the fair. They both wore gardening gloves and held sharp kitchen knives, which they used to cut fully grown pumpkins off of their vines.

Just as Debra was about to open her mouth with some complaint about where on earth Stephanie could be this time, and how they needed her help, and blah blah blah, a giant water balloon nailed her in the cheek, splattering orange paint all over her face and hair. She looked off into the distance to see Steph, still wearing her red plaid pajama pants and blue Mathletes sweatshirt, standing just outside the house. Next to her was a two-meter-tall wooden trebuchet on wheels and a red wagon full of water balloons.

"Stephanie! Get over here!" Debra shouted at the top of her lungs.

"Sorry, Mom! I didn't mean to hit you! I gotta work on my aim." Steph's far-away voice was muffled.

"Get over here *now*!" Debra repeated.

Steph walked out to the middle of the pumpkin patch, holding a spiral-bound notebook in her hands and leaving her wagon and trebuchet behind.

"Now, what in the good Lord's name are you doing?"

Steph exercised every ounce of self-control in her body to stifle the laughter she felt coming on when she looked at Debra's half-orange face. "I'm sorry, Mom. I honestly didn't mean to hit you. I was aiming for a tree on the other side of the yard. I think I might have calculated an angle wrong..." Steph glanced down at her notes, which were full of equations she'd learned in AP Physics and diagrams of projectile motion. "Yeah. I did. I see how to fix it. Sorry about that."

As Steph turned to walk back toward the house, Debra reached out and grabbed her shoulder to stop her. "That doesn't answer my question. What are you *doing*?"

"Oh, it's just a... *thing*..."

"That thing is *cool*!" Lizzie interjected, standing up and brushing the dirt off her knees.

"Thanks, Lizzie," said Steph.

"Okay, but for the third time, *what is it*?" asked Debra.

"I think I get it!" Lizzie shouted. "Orange paint! Orange like pumpkins. Because women are people, not pumpkins!"

Steph raised her hand and high-fived Lizzie.

"What is that supposed to *mean*, though?" asked Debra.

"Don't worry about it, Mom," said Steph.

"Well, forgive me, but when I have orange paint all over my face at 6:30 in the morning, I'm suddenly worried about it." She grabbed Steph's hand. "You're coming inside with me. We can talk about this while I wash off my face. Lizzie, keep cutting the vines."

In the kitchen, Steph sat at the small circular table with her notebook in front of her. Debra, still wearing her gardening gloves, stood at the sink, wiping her face off with a damp paper towel.

"You haven't been helping out on the farm at all. You've been disappearing every morning to go to that math club—"

"The *Mathletes*. And you've never *once* come to watch me—"

"You've been acting out—"

"Acting out of *what*? I'm one of the top students in my class."

"Then where did you get that... that *thingy*? Why is it that the *first* time I actually see you on the farm in the morning, you're launching water balloons? Help me out here, Steph, because I don't get it. Is it because of the pageant tomorrow? Are you nervous or something?"

Steph paused for a deep breath. "Do you hear me when I talk? Do you, Mom? Ever?"

Debra finished kneading the last few bits of paint out of her hair with the towel in her hands. "Sometimes I want to ask you the same question."

"Okay, well then let me be as clear with you as I can. I. Am. *Not*. Entering. The. Pageant. I have not signed up for it. I do not have a dress for it. I did not write a speech. When you see the girls on the stage at the fair tomorrow, I will not be among them. Do I need to word this differently? Am I getting through?"

"Yes, Stephanie," Debra sighed. "I hear you, okay? I know you don't want to do the pageant. But I don't get why you won't just *try* it. Keep an open mind. How do you know you won't like something you've never even tried?"

"Maybe because I'm capable of extrapolating? And you seem to be totally ignoring that I have *moral objections* to the pageant based on its inherent misogyny—"

"Not the big words, Steph, please," Debra held up a hand, signaling for Steph to stop talking. "I'm sorry, I just can't handle all your vocabulary right now."

"And that's another thing!" Steph yelled. She could feel her voice starting to break as the tears formed in her eyes. She blinked. "Why are you always trying to discourage me from being smart?"

Debra, shocked by Steph's sudden change in tone, took a seat across from her at the kitchen table. She slid the gloves off of her hands and looked Stephanie in the eyes. "What do you mean?"

"I study *so* hard. I've *always* worked hard at just about *everything.* Everything except being pretty. So it's like it doesn't even matter to you."

"Oh, honey." Debra reached across the table and put her hand on top of Steph's. "That's not it. I just don't want you to get hurt."

"So *you* decided to be as hurtful as possible to me instead?"

"No! No, of course not. I never wanted to hurt you. I just wanted to protect you. Look, it's okay to have dreams. You just seem to dream a little too big sometimes. And that's not to say that I don't believe in you, it's just that... Life can be full of disappointments, okay? And often, we don't do enough to prepare ourselves in case of failure. Which, to me, means getting to enjoy your glory days while they're here. High school, competing for Fair Queen... I don't want you to miss out on any of that."

"But to me, that's not glory," said Steph. "I want *my* glory days to be getting my acceptance letter to MIT. Or studying things I'm passionate about in college. Or working toward being a professor—"

"I know, sweetie." Debra patted Steph's hand and nodded along with the rhythm. "I know. I just don't want you to get your hopes up only to be crushed later on. Trust me, I know a thing or two about how that feels."

Steph nodded as well. For the first time in her life, she felt like she was starting to understand where her mother was coming from. "If I go to MIT, that doesn't mean I'm gonna leave you behind, Mom. I'm not like Dad was. I promise."

"Thank you, Stephanie. I appreciate that." The two of them shared a brief moment of silence before Debra added, "Now are you finally going to tell me what you were doing with that big wooden contraption outside?"

"Oh, my trebuchet. I built it in the garage last night."

"Yes, but *for what purpose*?"

"To show the town of Grey Acres that women are people, not pumpkins!" Lizzie called, pumping her fist in the air as she walked in from outside, layers of dirt caked all over her knees.

"If one of you doesn't tell me exactly what's going on right now, you're both grounded for the weekend." Debra paused. "Steph, that means you have to watch the pageant with me, and Lizzie, that means I won't let you enter any of your own pumpkins."

"Lizzie's right," said Steph. "The orange paint was symbolic. Last night, I saw a picture of one of our pumpkins wearing a Best in Show sash, and it looked too similar to your Fair Queen picture. The paint was meant to make a statement on how this town needs to stop judging women the way it judges pumpkins. You know, on appearance and stuff."

"Stephanie... am I understanding you correctly? You were planning to take that thing to the pageant with you?"

"And fling orange water balloons at the stage and the judges, yes."

"It's brilliant," Lizzie cackled.

"It's... *mean*," said Debra.

"Oh, but Grey Acres treating women like produce isn't?"

"What about the young women who *like* the pageant, Steph?" asked Debra. "The women like me. What are *you* treating *us* like?"

Steph froze for a moment. She realized that, for the first time in years, she actually saw Debra's point.

"What about us girls that *like* the pageant?" Katie asked, loudly slamming Jackie's locker shut to get his attention.

"Excuse me?" Jackie had slept terribly the night before. After falling asleep on the couch, he kept waking up about every hour or so and checking his phone to see if Logan had contacted him with any kind of apology or offer to make up. He'd even sent a few "Let's work this out" texts of his own to

Logan, all of which went unanswered. That meant one of two things: Logan was either ignoring him, or he'd slept peacefully through all the texts. Both options hurt. Now, seeing an angry Katie Thomas, whose dad had caused him a three-dollar deduction from his paycheck, put the icing on top of his already terrible morning.

"What were you doing at the convenience store last night?"

"Um... my job? Like I do every day?"

"No, dummy. I mean getting in a fight with my dad. I *told* you to stop, and you just kept going. Do you get off on making a scene or something?"

"What are you talking about? I was *defending* you."

"Defending me against *what*?"

"Against your dad being a big dick and not letting you get ice cream. And by the way, I got the cost of your sister's ice cream cone taken out of my paycheck for causing that scene. I thought you'd be thankful."

Katie's eyes grew wide. "Thankful for *what*? Humiliating me in public?" She shook her head. "And for the record, my dad wasn't *not letting* me have ice cream. I can make my own decisions about what I eat, thank you. He knew that I had *chosen* to go on a diet before the pageant, and was just trying to explain it to my sister."

Jackie nodded. "I'm sorry, Katie. I guess I didn't realize—"

"That women aren't all delicate little flowers being forced into things by men? That we don't all need *you* to defend us with what *you* think is in our best interest?"

"Look, I didn't mean it like—"

"You're just like Steph." Katie rolled her eyes, then pivoted away from Jackie.

"What's that supposed to mean?" Jackie called, but Katie was already walking away.

After a morning of being ignored by Logan in the hallway, then being ignored by Logan in Mr. Kowalski's history class, Jackie braced himself for a lunch period of being ignored by Logan in the cafeteria.

He sat at a table with his usual potato chips and usual can of Mountain Dew, but the lump in his throat told him that nothing felt right without his usual lunch buddy. At one point, he saw Logan walking toward his table with a tray full of chicken parmesan. Jackie considered calling out to him, but, not wanting to draw attention to the fact that his best friend was ignoring him, chose to wave him over instead. He knew Logan saw his little wave, too; Logan even turned his head and locked eyes with Jackie, keeping perfect eye contact as he walked away.

Jackie sighed and lowered his head, which narrowed his vision to nothing but a generic-brand bag of potato chips. When he finally looked back up a moment later, Logan was gone. He glanced back down at the potato chips, but the new, hot, stinging feeling in his stomach had stripped him of all hunger.

"Spill it!" Steph shouted, once she and Logan were safely behind the closed door of an empty classroom.

Logan nodded at his chicken parmesan. "Spill what? My tray of food? I knew you said we'd be playing dirty, but this was beyond what I expected."

Steph rolled her eyes. "I see you have Jackie's dumb sense of humor."

"Says the girl whose entire protest slogan was a pun on the word 'unfair'."

"Logan, I slept for zero hours and zero minutes last night. I am running on two 20-ounce coffees from Paul's Pancake World and pure, unadulterated passion. You do *not* want to mess with me right now."

Logan chuckled. "Remind me, Steph, is it pumpkins you raise, or drama llamas? 'Cause you're being a bit of a drama llama." Steph's face stayed locked in a flat, expressionless stare. Logan rolled his eyes. "Calm down, Steph. I'll tell you Jackie's plan, okay? But not because I want anything to do with any of this. Because you and Jackie are fighting for the same damn thing, and I, as a college-bound young gentleman with a bright future ahead of me, cannot stand to waste any more of my time on this stupid fight."

Steph nodded as she slowly slid her body into one of the classroom's chairs. "I'm listening."

Jackie recalled the bittersweet feeling he'd gotten back on his sixteenth birthday, when he'd first found his nametag in the Fine Jewelry box. He was feeling it again as he stood behind the deli counter at the convenience store, fumbling with the strings on his dark green apron the same way he did every afternoon as he tried to tie it behind his back before a shift. A bitterness for being stuck behind the counter for his three-hour Friday afternoon shift, and a sweetness for being able to escape all the drama, even if only for a few hours. Actually, the more Jackie thought about it, these three hours could be quite productive, if he properly seized the opportunities that would be literally standing right in front of him.

"What's your favorite thing about Grey Acres?" Jackie asked his first customer of the afternoon, a white-haired, saggy looking man wearing tan tweed slacks and a wrinkled green button-down.

"Why, the fair, of course!" the man answered. "The fair's been around since before I was even your age."

Considering this was the fair's 94th year, Jackie had certainly assumed that was the case, unless it meant Grey Acres's average lifespan was now somehow drastically increasing. "Thank you, sir," said Jackie.

"Are you going to make my sandwich?" the man asked. His voice was quiet and hoarse, like he was struggling to get the sounds out.

"Oh." Jackie looked down at the unsliced roll in front of him, and suddenly remembered he had an actual job to do.

By the second hour of his shift, though, Jackie had picked up some momentum, and the whole multi-tasking thing was coming to him much more easily.

"What's your favorite thing about Grey Acres?" Jackie asked a plump middle-aged woman with a frizzy brown bob. He threw two slices of salami onto a wheat roll, then reached for the Provolone.

"School district's pretty good," she said, shrugging.

Jackie nodded and sprinkled chopped lettuce on the sandwich. He closed the bun, wrapped the sandwich in tinfoil, and placed it on the counter in front of him. "Thanks for your help," he said. Frizzy Bob Lady shrugged again, took her sandwich off the counter, and headed for the cash register. The next customer, a lanky man with tired-looking eyes, approached him.

"What kind of sandwich can I get you, and what's your favorite thing about Grey Acres?" Jackie asked in his best car-salesman voice.

"What?" asked the lanky man. "I mean, turkey and Swiss. And I guess I like that the mall's so close. Why?"

"Just writing a speech about Grey Acres," Jackie replied as he placed thin slices of turkey on a bun.

"Well, okay, then," said the lanky man.

Just then, Jackie watched the lanky man suddenly stumble to his side as Steph pushed past him and emerged from the back of the line.

"Footlong meatball sub," she announced as she reached the counter.

"Um, take a look behind you," said Jackie. "There's a line." He waved his hand forward, gesturing to the long line of customers behind her.

"That's not important. I need to talk to you," she said. "When do you get off?"

"Um, how about when I'm looking at pictures of your *mom*?"

An audible *gasp* came from an old woman in the middle of the line.

"I'm sorry, ma'am," Jackie called to her. "Didn't mean that the way it sounded."

Steph chuckled. "You totally did. Anyway, smarty pants, when does your shift end?"

"Six," said Jackie.

"Great. Meet you on the roof then. Bring the meatball sub." Steph, with one swift pivot, turned herself away from Jackie, and confidently strode out of the store.

"That's gonna cost you four dollars!" Jackie called after her, but Steph never looked back.

At six, the sky was in its transition stage, leaving it in that weird limbo between light blue and navy. It almost looked grey. Jackie had considered blowing Steph off and not showing up on the roof after all she'd put him through, but some part of him at least wanted to hear what she had to say. (He'd decided he definitely wasn't bringing the meatball sub, though.)

When Jackie saw Steph sitting cross-legged on the roof, elbows resting on her knees and head resting in her hands, he suddenly felt that same little nauseous jolt he'd been feeling all day. He hoisted his body up off the ladder and planted his feet firmly on the roof, then walked toward Steph. "Logan usually sits there," he said.

"I know," said Steph, nodding. "It's where you guys usually meet, right?"

"How'd you know that?" Jackie, still standing, asked. "Are you and Erin in cahoots with him on everything?"

Steph nodded again. "Just take a seat. Let's talk." For the first time since the pageant debacle began, Steph's voice was actually friendly.

Facing Steph, Jackie sat down cross-legged as well. "How much has Logan told you?" he asked.

"Everything," Steph replied.

"Wow," Jackie sighed. "I can't believe he actually betrayed me."

"He didn't. He just told me that you and I have a common goal."

"You want to destroy the pageant. I can't win the pageant if you destroy it. Also, now that Logan's given you that precious information, please don't go using it to get me disqualified. I don't want to be part of your cause."

Steph shook her head. "You're not getting it. Of course I'm not going to get you disqualified."

Jackie's eyebrows furrowed in curiosity.

"We both want this town to *change*, Jackie."

"Ah." Jackie nodded. "So I guess Logan hasn't told you *everything*, then. He hasn't told you how apparently, at least according to him, I don't give two shits about change, and all I care about is boosting my own image for college. I guess Logan left out the part where I'm a major self-centered asshole who doesn't have any real passion for anything, right?"

Steph bowed her head as she broke into a fit of giggles.

"What's funny about this?"

"Jesus Christ, Jackie," said Steph. "If all you cared about was standing out to colleges, you could've joined, like, the environmental club or something. Or done, like, one term on student council. Or, just written some really meaningful essay about, I don't know, how making sandwiches for the horrible people of Grey Acres changed your perspective on humanity or whatever. Instead, you chose to do something that's *literally* never been done before in this town. You almost stole a prom dress from the town's only department store in the middle of the afternoon. You sent your eight-year-old brother to commit grand theft pumpkin on my sister. You even risked losing your best friend. If that's not passion, Jackie, I don't know *what* is."

Jackie, in his silence, found himself nodding along with Steph's words. When she stopped talking, he just stared at her for a moment. For the first time since their whole mess started, she was actually smiling. And she was actually making sense. "So, here we are then, I guess. Just two super passionate people, sitting on the rooftop of a convenience store on the eve of the day the pageant... what? Gets destroyed?"

Steph shook her head. "No. After talking to my mom this morning, and talking to Logan this afternoon... I've decided I'm not gonna destroy the pageant anymore."

Jackie's eyes grew wide. He felt a cold rush of relief washing over him. "You're not?"

"Nope," she said. "I'm gonna enter it with you."

Chapter Seven

Saturday Morning

The usually empty land that sat adjacent to Almond's Convenience Store wasn't so empty anymore. Giant tents draped in large white plastic awnings covered the grounds. Some tents housed tables of competing fruits and vegetables, while others held numbered cows and goats. Food vendor trucks, which featured just the classics—Crunchy's Chicken, Paul's Pancake World, and Asian Smoothies—lined the grass that bordered the road. In between a few tents sat an inflatable orange bouncy castle and a meager six-foot rock-climbing wall. Gus Bennett of Gus's Supermarket drove his tractor, which pulled a trailer full of hay bales and squealing children through the fairground. In the center of it all stood a large wooden stage followed by dozens of rows of folding chairs. The stage was adorned with a set of royal blue curtains, as well as a mustard yellow banner, hand-painted by the Grey Acres High School theatre department, that read "94th Annual Fair Queen Pageant" in loopy blue script.

Jackie felt his heart nervously flitting around in his chest as he and his family passed the stage on their walk through the fair. Jack Sr. and Heather, walking a couple paces in front of their kids, held hands and mumbled to each other about which tents they'd have to visit that day. Jackie didn't see any reason for their mumbling. Of course they'd visit every tent. There was literally nothing else to do within a ten-mile radius.

Jackie took each step carefully. Each time his foot hit the ground and he heard the little *squish* of grass and mud beneath it, he had to check to make sure his dress shoes remained clean. He stepped lightly throughout the field, cautious of any mud splattering up onto the cuffs of his pants. For the first time in his life, Jackie was wearing a full three-piece suit, which he'd borrowed from his father. Jack Sr. hadn't gone to a formal event in quite some time, he'd told Jackie, which is why neither of them were surprised when the suit fit Jackie perfectly. Jack Sr. had been more than a little confused as to why Jackie wanted to wear a suit to the Town Fair, of all places, but Jackie had just brushed it off by claiming he had a surprise for his parents. Jackie had never done much in the way of surprising them before, so Jack Sr. and Heather both excitedly went along with it. And why shouldn't they? Jackie figured that watching their son rock it at a beauty pageant was at *least* as good of a surprise as a nametag in a Fine Jewelry box.

Since Jack Sr. and Heather were wandering into the cow tent to explore on their own, and Jackie was busy reviewing the Fair Queen speech he'd written on his hand, Terry made his own way into one of the vegetable tents.

Lizzie was already in the tent, placing a bright orange, perfectly spherical pumpkin onto a white-clothed table for judging. "Simon family pumpkins are the *best best best*," Lizzie sang under her breath. She reached into the back pocket of her denim overalls and pulled out a white folded index card. "Lizzie Simon, Age 8. Pumpkin Extraordinaire," it read. Lizzie quietly chuckled a little. "Bet Terry can't spell 'extraordinaire,'" she whispered to herself.

"Hola, señorita!" A familiar little boy's voice broke through Lizzie's ego-inflating session. She whipped her head around, causing her long brown braids to fling around her head in a propeller-like motion, and saw Terry standing in front of her, holding a wimpy little plant in his hands.

Terry placed his "plant," a ceramic pot of soil with a tiny green sprout peeking out from the dirt, on the display table next to Lizzie's perfect pumpkin.

"What's *that* supposed to be?" Lizzie snorted.

"Una calabaza," Terry replied.

"In *English*, dummy."

"It's a pumpkin, mi amor."

Lizzie rolled her eyes. "You call *that* a pumpkin? What a *loser*."

"It's just not done growing yet," Terry explained. "But look. It's still happy!" He turned the pot around so its Sharpie-drawn smiley face was staring straight at Lizzie.

"In case you didn't get the memo, Almond, this is a contest for pumpkins that are *already* grown."

Terry nodded. "I know. You'll win."

Lizzie skeptically narrowed her eyes. "And you're *okay* with that?"

"Yeah," shrugged Terry. "Pumpkins are your life. You deserve it."

"But I thought you were supposed to be my *rival*! I thought you were *competing* with me—"

"Nah. I just wanted an excuse to get your attention."

"Why?"

A huge smile spread across Terry's face. "¡Porque *te amo*, señorita!" he shouted, throwing his arms in the air.

"You're a weird kid, Almond," laughed Lizzie.

Meanwhile, Jackie wove through a maze of greasy-faced, Crunchy's-Chicken-eating children as he made his way toward the bouncy castle. Every few seconds, he glanced at his cell phone, which showed a few texts from Steph about meeting him behind the bouncy castle at noon. Jackie had sent Logan a few texts throughout the morning asking him if they could meet at the fair and talk, all of which had gone unanswered. He knew logically that continually checking his phone wouldn't increase the chances that Logan would respond, but something in his brain kept giving his hands the urge to check it anyway.

As Jackie passed the Paul's Pancake World food truck, he noticed a small folding table next to it, with a banner reading "Feinstein's Department Store" draped across the front. Logan and Ronald stood behind the table, handing out coupons to passersby. Nervously sliding his hands into his pockets, Jackie approached the table.

"Hey, Logan," he mumbled. "I, uh, sent you a few texts. I was wondering if there was a time today we could—"

"Fifteen percent off your next purchase of $30 or more," said Logan, thrusting a coupon toward Jackie's face.

Jackie took the coupon. "I know you're probably still mad at me," he said. "But I think we can work this—"

"Or you can sign up for the mailing list," Logan said, holding up a clipboard full of handwritten names and addresses. "Then you'll get great deals like this every week."

Jackie pursed his lips and nodded to himself. He glanced down at the coupon, which featured bright-red lettering, a glossy finish, and pictures of suit jackets and prom dresses. He chuckled softly.

"You know, prom's still not til May," he said, trying to smile a little as he pointed to a prom dress on the coupon.

Logan glanced over at Ronald, who was busy talking two plump middle-aged women in fleece sweaters into signing up for the mailing list. He leaned in toward Jackie and lowered his voice. "Look, I wasn't even gonna come to the fair today. I'm really not interested in watching you or Steph get into whatever shenanigans you're planning to pull, okay? I just want to hand out some coupons with my dad, receive $50 from my dad for spending all day handing out said coupons, maybe get an Asian Smoothie if I'm feeling it, then go home and read some Hemingway."

"Because Hemingway makes everyone feel better, right? Hemingway is the best medicine, second only to laughter." Jackie attempted to put on his most convincing playful voice.

Logan rolled his eyes. "Notice that *none* of the things I mentioned involve you."

The fleece-sweater ladies finished signing up for the mailing list and handed the clipboard back to Ronald. Ronald almost handed the clipboard to Jackie, but then quickly rescinded it.

"Did you give him a coupon?" he asked Logan.

"Yeah, Dad, but—"

Ronald snatched the coupon out of Jackie's hand. "No. Hooligans who run around my store in women's formalwear don't get my discounts. Especially not those who try to steal from me."

"Look, Mr. Feinstein, I wasn't trying to steal. I was just running out of the store so fast, and I didn't even realize—"

"*There* you are!" a voice shouted, cutting Jackie off. He whipped his head around to see Steph running toward him. "I thought we were going to meet at the bouncy castle." She grabbed his arm and pulled him away from the Feinsteins. "Come on. It's already after noon."

Chapter Eight

Saturday Afternoon

After Steph had pulled Jackie away from the Feinstein's Department Store table, she immediately let go of his arm. "Walk with me. Don't draw attention to yourself."

"That's a little difficult when I'm already wearing a suit."

"Sucks to be you," laughed Steph, who was wearing her usual outfit of faded jeans, a blue Mathletes sweatshirt, and chunky brown boots. She also wore a roll of beige masking tape around her left hand like a bracelet.

Jackie pulled his phone out of his pocket to check the time. "Okay, so it's 12:03." He looked up from the cell phone screen to see people from all around the fair filing into the large white vegetable tent. "There's, what, like 20 categories to announce?"

"Yeah, at least. We should have about half an hour."

Jackie and Steph reached the makeshift wooden stage where, in a few short hours, the pageant would be happening. Steph whipped a measuring tape out of the front pocket of her sweatshirt. "Let's get to work."

"Vegetable contest, category one!" Marvin Flounder boomed into the battery-operated microphone he held in his right hand, his nasal voice echoing throughout the tent. "Squash! Children ages ten and under! I will announce one honorable mention, two runner ups, and the winner!" Next to him stood a table of wimpy, bruised squashes.

"This is the guy that advises our kids at school?" Jack Sr. whispered in Heather's ear. "No wonder Jackie never listens to him." Heather playfully elbowed Jack Sr. in the ribs as Flounder announced the town's top young squash prodigies.

After a few kids from Grey Acres Elementary accepted their ribbons from Flounder, he began walking toward the children's pumpkin table. "Vegetable contest, category two!" he announced. "Pumpkins! Children ages ten and under!"

"He's gonna do this for *every* category, isn't he?" Jack Sr., giggling, whispered to Heather.

"And the honorable mention goes to... Terry Almond!"

Terry emerged from the middle of the crowd, excitedly skipping toward Flounder. "Gracias!" he exclaimed.

Flounder shook Terry's hand as he handed him a small white ribbon. "Your pumpkin may not be all there yet, but the judges thought it had a lot of personality."

"Sí," said Terry. "Es una calabaza de felicidad."

"Don't push it," said Flounder. He patted Terry on the back, but it wasn't so much a *congratulations* as it was a *get back into the audience; we're moving on.*

Terry walked back into the crowd, pushing past people until he reached Lizzie. "Guess I'm not such a loser after all," he said, holding up his ribbon. "I mean, you'll definitely get first place. But my happy little plant didn't totally lose either."

Lizzie smiled at Terry. "Yeah. I guess it didn't."

Steph held her end of the tape measure against the wooden stage, while Jackie walked away from her, pulling his end. "Stop when you reach three meters," said Steph.

Jackie watched the little numbers emerging from the tape measure increase with every step he took. "Right here!" he shouted. Steph tossed him the roll of masking tape from around her wrist. It flew in little circles in the air before descending straight into his open hands. "Nice throw!" he said.

"What can I say? I know my projectile motion."

Jackie chuckled, rolled his eyes, and knelt on the ground with the roll of masking tape. Right where the tape measure read three meters, he placed two pieces of masking tape on the ground in a small X. "Okay! That should be all of them!" Jackie stood up, holding his end of the tape measure in one hand and brushing the dirt off his knees with the other. A few meters to his left and to his right sat two other masking-tape Xs. "Now let's do my thing before my suit gets any dirtier."

Next thing he knew, he and Steph had vacated the pageant area and were running together toward Almond's Convenience Store.

"I'm surprised your dad closed up today," said Steph, a little out of breath from running. "You'd think the fair would be, like, Black Friday or something for him."

They slowed their pace as they reached the back door to Almond's.

"We used to stay open during the fair," said Jackie. He reached into the pocket of his suit pants and pulled out a key. "But then Paul of Paul's Pancake World got mad that we were taking his coffee sales away, then he wanted to start this movement to make people get licenses to sell food at the fair, and it became this whole thing. So my dad just kinda gave in." Jackie inserted the key into the doorknob and opened the door. He gestured for Steph to go ahead of him.

"Thanks," said Steph as Jackie held the door. He followed behind her. "I'm surprised he gave in so easily."

Jackie shrugged. "My dad's never been one to make waves. I guess I never was either. Until now, I mean."

"It's fun, isn't it?"

"It's... complicated."

"Fair," Steph nodded.

"That another one of your *puns*?" Jackie asked, smiling. Steph rolled her eyes and playfully pushed him forward, hard enough to cause him to take a few more steps toward the deli.

When Jackie reached the deli, he went behind the counter and pulled two aprons off of the hooks on the wall. He tossed one to Steph, which landed perfectly on her face. She pulled the apron off of her head, laughing as she tried to smooth down the hair it had ruffled. "Guess my projectile motion game's not bad either," said Jackie.

"Guess not," smiled Steph.

Jackie finished tying the apron strings behind his back. "Ready to make sandwiches?"

Chapter Nine
Saturday Evening

"Good evening, citizens of Grey Acres. I have an announcement to make," a dry, monotone voice loudly projected through the loudspeakers set up all around the fair. On the wooden pageant stage stood Timothy Peach, who had served as mayor of Grey Acres for the past ten years. It was obvious why, too; in his dark-wash khakis and charcoal blazer, and with his bland, passionless voice, Mayor Peach looked like the perfect personification of the town. Glancing at Janice Hooper, who was standing directly to his left, Mayor Peach said into his microphone, "It is now five o'clock. Please make your way toward the stage for the ninety-fourth annual Grey Acres Fair Queen Pageant."

People began emerging from all over the fair. Exhausted-looking parents dragged their screaming children out of the bouncy castle. Teenagers left the food trucks carrying Asian Smoothies or Paul's maple syrup lattes. Town residents scrubbed the layers of Crunchy's Chicken grease off of their faces with thin white napkins that almost tore from the weight of the grease after every swipe. As everyone moved toward the center of the field and into the folding chairs facing the wooden stage, Mayor Peach continued his announcement. "This year's pageant judges will consist of the following people: Mr. Leland Kowalski of Grey Acres High School; Mrs. Mary Ann Pegsworth of Grey Acres Elementary School; and Miss Noelle Northberger, of the Grey Acres Mall's very own Nails by Noelle Northberger."

The three judges, sitting in folding chairs in the first row, turned around to wave at the growing audience. Mayor Peach handed the microphone over to Janice Hooper and exited the stage.

Janice Hooper, wearing the same 1940s floor-length evening gown she wore every year (including the years *she* competed in the pageant), now stood center-stage, holding the microphone in her frail, bony hand. The microphone bobbed up and down a little as her hand shook. "W-weeeeelcoooome to the Faaaaair Queeeen Beeeaauuuuuuty Paaaageant, nuuumber niiiinety-foooour." She took about half a minute to force out those words in her wimpy, hoarse little voice. "This pageant's been around longer than *I* have!" The crowd let out a hesitant laugh as the last few people finished taking their seats. Mrs. Hooper laughed along with them, the saggy skin along her throat flopping around with every exhale.

Eleven pageant contestants gathered backstage, which, in Grey Acres terms, just meant the patch of grass behind the stage's curtains. A few girls, with their hair freshly fried by a curling iron and their nails freshly painted by Noelle Northberger, paced back and forth in the grass, silently mouthing their speeches to themselves.

Becky Norman, with her dark-blonde hair intricately knotted in a pile on top of her head, used one hand to hold a small mirror up to her face, and the other to apply more and more coats of a lipstick she called "Fierce Fuchsia."

Katie Thomas was wearing the metallic-gold sequined ball gown Jackie had rejected from

Feinstein's Department Store. She was one of the girls pacing on the grass and silently practicing her speech, somehow maintaining perfect posture, despite her four-inch heels. Her concentration suddenly broke as she noticed Steph making her way into the group of girls. "What are *you* doing here?" Katie asked.

Steph, who was still wearing her faded jeans and Mathletes sweatshirt, pushed her trebuchet, covered in a bright-red floral-print vinyl tablecloth, toward the backstage area. "Same as you," she answered.

"You mean, after spending all this time acting like a huge pretentious asshole about the pageant, you actually decided to enter it?"

Steph shrugged. "I can admit when I'm wrong."

Katie rolled her eyes. "Forgive me, but that hasn't really been your reputation."

"...Beeecccck-k-ky N-n-noooorman!" Janice Hooper's muffled voice sounded from the stage. Becky blew the other contestants a kiss and parted the curtains as she skipped onto the stage.

In the audience sat a few hundred Grey Acres residents. Logan sat in the back row, still holding sign-up sheets for the department store mailing list.

Logan had been hoping he'd be free to go before the pageant began, but he knew his dad would never want to pass up a marketing opportunity as good as an event with the better part of the town present. "I'll take the left side. You take the right," Ronald Feinstein had said while he gathered the remaining coupons and sign-up sheets from their table, then immediately started ushering Logan to follow him. Logan untensed his muscles as he felt himself letting go of the last glimmer of hope that he might be able to leave the fair early.

Now, Logan held the sign-up sheet on a clipboard in his lap, and busied himself trying to balance a pencil on his nose while he watched Becky take the stage.

"Some of you may remember me as last year's Fair Queen," said Becky. "And you'd be right."

Logan rolled his eyes. What was that, a joke? A really reflexive statement? He wondered if Becky ever spent time thinking about how her words actually sounded out loud, or if she just enjoyed stringing clichés together for the hell of it.

"But I'm back for more. Because the truth is, I can't get enough of this wonderful town. Last year I said that this town's best attribute wasn't its economy, school district, or agriculture, but its *people*. And I'll stand by that. The folks of Grey Acres are fiercer than the fuchsia on my lips!"

"Shut *up*, Becky!" Logan muttered under his breath. Despite how much he lowered his voice, his words still somehow echoed. Or, at least sounded like they echoed.

"Jinx, I guess?" said Erin, turning around in her seat to face Logan.

"That was you?"

Erin nodded.

"Erin, real quick, now that we're speaking again, I just wanted to apologize—"

She shook her head. "Don't worry about it. Sometimes we do stupid things for our friends when they need us. I might have a little first-hand experience with that myself."

"I was kinda hoping that *we* could be friends too, though. I still need someone to talk about books with, if you can forgive me?"

A male arm from the seat next to Erin wrapped itself around her shoulders. "I don't know. Friends with a *guy*? Might make *me* a little jealous." Laughing a little, the boy craned his neck to face Logan. Logan noticed a signature red bow tie affixed to the front of the boy's white dress shirt. He was probably the only person other than Jackie to dress that nice for the fair.

"Oh, Logan, you know Aaron, right?" said Erin. "He asked me to go to the fair with him yesterday."

Aaron shrugged. "Figured, I might as well give the Aaron-and-Erin thing a try. Plus, it was awesome to find someone who still believes in bringing dates to the fair."

"Right back at you," said Erin. They nuzzled noses. Logan sat back in his seat, wondering if he was living in an episode of *The Twilight Zone*. (Especially since Grey Acres had always seemed like a perfect backdrop for that type of story.)

"When you asked me to sign that petition, I felt like I was in some kind of twilight zone or something." Katie still faced Steph backstage. "I mean, I've been the Fair Queen runner-up *two years in a row* now. How much do you think I hate myself?"

"I honestly didn't know you were the runner-up."

"Of course." Katie breathed out a sarcastic little laugh. "You *couldn't* have known that, because you don't know shit about the pageant. You never have."

"Well, now I'm trying to learn more. Just give me a little credit."

"Honestly, it's hard to. Especially when you show up to one of Grey Acres's oldest traditions wearing *that*."

Steph shrugged. "I decided to focus more on the talent portion."

Katie glanced at Steph's trebuchet which, in its covering, looked more like an homage to a 1970s kitchen than anything recognizable. "I'm assuming that's why you brought this big... lump?... along with you?"

Steph nodded.

"What is it, anyway?"

"You'll see."

Under the tablecloth, Jackie, who held a drawstring bag in his lap, sat cross-legged in between the trebuchet's planks. His back was starting to ache from spending so long hunched over, and his neck was getting sore from holding his head down so it wouldn't collide with the wood. He could feel his legs getting stiff from contracting his muscles in order to stay perfectly still. He didn't want to risk wrinkling—or worse, tearing—his suit. His plan was to remain hidden in the trebuchet until he was called onstage. That way, he didn't risk anyone exposing his plan, and possibly disqualifying him, before he had the chance to wow the judges.

"Can I see *now*?" asked Katie.

"No."

"Why not?"

"What do you mean *why not*? It's *my* talent. It's covered for a reason."

Katie scoffed. "How dumb do you think I *am*, Steph? I mean, I always knew you thought girls like me were stupider and more easily manipulated by the patriarchy than yourself, but really. Exactly *how* dumb do you take me for?"

"I never said you were dumb."

"You didn't have to. I know what you're doing. You have some kind of 'secret weapon' under that cloth that you're going to use to somehow destroy the entire pageant once you're actually up on stage. God, you have no shame, do you?"

"That's not true, Katie."

"Then show me what's under the cloth."

"No." Steph stepped in front of her covered trebuchet and wrapped her arms backwards around it, forming a protective shield.

Katie's arm lunged forward as she made a grabbing motion at the cloth. Steph swatted Katie's arm away, which, considering Katie's four-inch heels, easily knocked her off balance. She fell backwards into the grass, landing straight on her butt.

"Oh my God." Katie hoisted herself up with her arms, then stood up slowly as she tried to regain balance in her heels. She quickly turned her head to glance at the back of her dress, only to find her butt covered in grade-A fertile Grey Acres farm soil.

"Katie, I am so sorry. I did not mean to—"

"Save it." Katie pushed her dirt-covered hands into Steph's shoulders, knocking her into the trebuchet she was guarding. The force of Steph's body hitting the trebuchet set its wheels in motion. The ground's slight decline made the trebuchet roll away from Steph, slowly gaining momentum.

"K-kaaaatie Thooomaaasss." At the cue of Janice Hooper's voice, Katie quickly brushed off the back of her dress the best she could and rushed out onto the stage.

Steph followed the rolling trebuchet. She lunged forward, reaching to grab a plank of wood under the tablecloth. Instead, she just hit the trebuchet head-on again, this time knocking it over.

"Ow!" yelled Jackie, whose shout was accompanied by a few loud *snap*s and *thunk*s as he fell onto his side.

Steph swiftly whisked the tablecloth off of Jackie and the trebuchet. She tossed it off to the side and knelt down next to Jackie. "Are you all right?"

Jackie nodded, but still let out a few painful exhales as he climbed out from between the planks of wood, dragging his draw-string bag with him. Now free from his hiding place, he let himself fall to his knees in the grass. "God*damn* it," he muttered when he saw the tear in his suit pants and his newly grass-stained knee.

Steph, still kneeling down next to her trebuchet, gingerly ran her hands along the planks as she inspected the damage. A few planks snapped in half, and many of those that hadn't were at least a little bent. "Rest in peace, Lorelai," she whispered.

"You named that thing?" Jackie asked.

Steph nodded. "How are your sandwiches?"

Jackie opened the drawstring bag and looked inside. The foil-wrapped sandwiches had gotten a little smooshed in the fall, but Jackie figured people wouldn't care. Nobody really cares about that kind of thing when they're getting free food. "They're okay, I guess."

Steph glanced over at the backstage area, which they were now a few yards away from. While most of the contestants were still wrapped up in their own heads, practicing their speeches and strutting back and forth through the grass, a few were staring confusedly at her and Jackie.

"I guess I have to think up a whole new act now," sighed Steph.

That's when they both heard a faint hissing noise coming from toward the stage. "Ssssss," it said. Then it got louder. "Sssssssssteeephanie S-s-s-siiiiimon." It was Janice Hooper.

Chapter Ten
Saturday Night

To the cadence of sparse, unenthused applause, Steph parted the curtains and stepped forward onto the stage. Though her hair was tied back in a ponytail, a few pieces had recently escaped, creating a thin layer of frizz around her skull. The knees of her faded blue jeans were now deeply stained with grass and dirt. She nervously glanced out at the audience, then at the grass to the side of the stage, where Becky and Katie were confidently standing, occasionally smiling at waving at random audience members. Steph drew a deep breath.

"I'm the face of Grey Acres," she said. "I'm a hard worker with big dreams, just like a lot of people I meet in this town. Like, I see so many people in this town devoting their lives to their restaurants or their department stores, their convenience stores or their pumpkin farms... and a lot of girls who work really hard at being amazing at this pageant. Like Becky, or Katie, or my mom."

Steph looked out into the audience, where she saw Debra and Lizzie sitting in the front row. Even though she knew Debra would never miss the pageant for anything short of a nuclear bomb threat, something still felt nice about finally seeing her mom in the audience. Next to Debra, Lizzie smiled up at Steph, absentmindedly stroking her blue-ribbon-adorned pumpkin with her left hand.

"I know you all probably think I'm a little intense. And you'd be right."

Logan and Erin simultaneously let out a soft laugh. "See, Steph knows how to actually use that phrase correctly," Logan whispered. Erin nodded, giggling a little under her breath.

"But we're all a little intense, aren't we? I mean, when we really, *really* want something? Isn't that just what *passion* is?"

Steph paused for a moment and glanced to her right. If all had gone as planned, her trebuchet would have been standing in the blank space next to her. Jackie would have snuck out from under the tablecloth as she wheeled it onstage, and slipped in between two curtain folds, where he would have hidden until it was his turn.

"What I'm passionate about is math," she continued. "Everyone who's met me probably knows that at this point. Tomorrow I'm sending in my application to MIT. Then, if all goes well, I'll get to be a professor when I grow up. I work hard for the things I care about, just like you guys." She paused for a moment as a lump began to form in her throat. She swallowed hard. "I had a big thing planned for the talent portion, but it got destroyed just a few minutes ago. Look down at the grass."

She watched as everyone in the audience bent their heads downward and looked at the ground.

"Three of you should have masking-tape Xs under your chairs. This was the part where I was going to ask those people to move themselves and their chairs out of the way. It would've been, like, an audience-participatory talent portion or something. And then I had this, like, two-meter tall trebuchet that fired water balloons at targets. So I was going to shoot them right at the Xs and show you guys how accurate I made it by using the projectile motion equations we learned in AP Physics... Because, as lame as that may sound to a lot of people, that's the kind of thing I like to do for fun. That's what I care about. The point is, I don't think the main thing the young women of this town should be judged on is physical appearance. Because to me, working hard at the things you care about, whether that's math, or pumpkins, or being pretty... whatever it is, *that's* what I think is beautiful. So that's why I'm the face of Grey Acres." A moment of awkward silence followed. "Thank you," Steph blurted out, realizing she needed to clearly indicate that she was done.

Light, sporadic clapping noises began emerging from the audience. Steph nodded, accepting her mediocre response, and started walking over to join Becky and Katie offstage.

That's when Erin leapt up out of her seat and started cheering at the top of her lungs as she loudly slapped her hands together. Boy Aaron did the same. Then Logan followed behind them.

Steph turned toward the audience. She saw Lizzie standing up in front of her chair, screaming, "*Woo-hoooooo*," as she performed a happy dance that involved shaking her pumpkin above her head.

Debra, who was clapping as well, made perfect eye contact with Steph as she nodded and gave her a small, genuine smile. Steph smiled and nodded back at Debra, then turned to her right and walked offstage.

"J-j-jjjj-jjjjjjaaaackie Aaaaalmond," called Janice Hooper. She looked back down at the list of names in her shaky hand, and a look of confusion overtook her eyebrows. "Wwwaaaaiiit, isn't Jaaaackie—"

"Good evening, Grey Acres!" Jackie called, bursting through the curtain.

A moment of silence washed over the crowd. Janice Hooper's eyes grew wide. Jackie faintly heard Jack Sr. whisper, "Whatever it costs to repair that suit is coming out of his paycheck."

"I guess we've got a quiet crowd tonight, so I figured I'd start by pumping everyone up with my talent portion!" He reached into his drawstring bag and started tossing foil-wrapped sandwiches out at the audience. A few townspeople leapt up to catch them. One sandwich hit Frizzy Bob Lady right in the face. Fortunately, most of the rest seemed to land in people's hands, outside of the few that managed to land in the dirt. Jackie silently mourned the sandwich casualties, but continued his presentation.

"Right now, that's my talent," he said. "I make sandwiches. You've probably all bought one from me at some time or another over the past two years."

He stared out at the crowd, who still stared silently back at him. He heard one lady whisper, "Isn't this kinda thing why Paul wanted food vendors to have licenses?"

Jackie's blood pressure rose a little as he realized that he might not be ready for a lackluster response. He stared at his hand, which started to shake Janice-Hooper-style, as he studied the words to his speech. The black ink that had formed the letters was now slightly faded due to multiple rounds of hand-washing throughout his sandwich-making process earlier. Finally, Jackie dropped his hand to his side. "I'm gonna be real with you guys," he said. "I agree with Becky. The best part about this town isn't its school district or economy or whatever. Most towns probably have high schools of some kind. And our economy is shit."

Flounder audibly gasped from the third row.

"Sorry, Mr. Flounder. I mean, our economy is high-quality Grey Acres crop fertilizer. But we do have one thing going for us. Which is that sometimes I see signs that we're willing to improve, willing to change. Like take Steph, for example." Jackie gestured to the line of girls gathered at the side of the stage. "I knew literally no one who hated this pageant more than she did. But when she found a new angle to view it from, she decided to give it a try." He glanced over at Steph, who smiled back at him.

Then, he scanned the crowd to find Logan, who was boredly shuffling the pile of department store coupons in his lap. Jackie stared right at him. "I'm trying to improve myself, too. I know I haven't been the best friend this past week. Logan, I'm sorry." Logan looked up from his stack of coupons and, for the first time in days, finally held eye contact with Jackie. "You were right. At first, my plan was to just enter the pageant so I'd look more well-rounded to colleges. But once we started on this whole crazy adventure, I realized it was a lot more than that." He briefly broke eye contact with Logan to address the crowd again. "Steph's right, you guys. This town is full of passionate people. I don't know exactly what my passion is yet. I'm at least eighty percent sure it's not making sandwiches or ice cream cones or cash register transactions. But I want to find out what it is. So that's where I'll conclude today. Over the past week, I've changed a lot as a person, and I know a lot of people in this town have the potential to as well. That's why I'm asking you to take a leap and try something that's never been done before. Accept me as your first male Fair Queen. Let me be the face of Grey Acres. Thank you." Jackie pivoted away from center-stage and walked toward the line of girls at the side, stepping to the cadence of the same scattered applause Steph received.

As he walked offstage, he craned his neck to see who was clapping. Both Jack Sr. and Heather held big grins on their faces as they clapped. Terry was even standing on his seat, and Jackie was pretty sure he heard him yell, "¡Muy hermosa, mi hermano!"

He looked to the back row, hoping to see one last person clapping. With a subtle grin on his face, Logan gave Jackie an approving nod. Jackie smiled back at him, then made his way into the line of contestants.

Of course, Becky Norman won the pageant again. But hey, it made sense; pageants were Becky's passion.

Chapter Eleven
Sunday Again

Hard work. Hard work and just being a nice guy. Until last week, that's all I thought mattered. Late-morning on Sunday, Jackie sat on his living-room couch with his notebook in his lap. This time, the ideas for his essay flowed much more easily out of him. The Spanish soap opera playing on the TV in front of him didn't even serve as that much of a distraction; he still didn't understand the language at all.

Terry sat in front of the TV in a daze as he watched the lives of his beloved soap opera characters play out in front of him. He held his plant in his lap, which now wore a white honorable-mention ribbon like a necktie under its Sharpie-drawn face. Terry lovingly stroked the leaves blooming out of the green sprouts.

Steph, not having slept much at all this past week, finally rolled out of bed around noon on Sunday. When she entered the kitchen, she found Debra sitting at the table in a blue terry-cloth bathrobe, leaning back in her chair and sipping coffee from a pumpkin-shaped mug. Steph was pretty sure she'd never seen Debra that relaxed before. Though Debra's change in demeanor was a pleasant morning surprise, Steph was even more surprised when she saw the orange gift-wrapped box sitting on the table.

"I'm proud of you, Stephanie."

Steph smiled at her mom, though a bit skeptically, since it wasn't a phrase she was that used to hearing. She slid into the chair across from her and looked down at the present. "What's this?"

"You wear the same sweatshirt almost every day," Debra said, gesturing to Steph's Mathletes sweatshirt, which she'd once again slept in. The color was starting to fade a little in the shoulders and elbows. A small tear had formed in the front pocket. "One of these days, you're going to wear it out."

Steph took a deep breath, preparing herself for another "I'm proud of you, but..." moment. "How is that relevant?" she asked.

Debra shrugged. "I just thought you could use a new sweatshirt."

Steph hesitantly grabbed the box off of the table and started tearing the wrapping paper off. After she'd finished removing it, she rolled it into a tight wrapping-paper ball and threw it across the room, toward the kitchen trash can. The paper ball sailed right in. Steph knew her projectile motion.

Now left with a cardboard box sitting in her lap, Steph lifted off the lid to find a brand-new dark red sweatshirt, the letters MIT stitched across the front. Steph gasped as a smile suddenly flew across her face. It was a weird sensation for her, since she never saw herself as the kind of person who could gasp in excitement. She looked up at Debra with smiling eyes, speechless.

Debra took another sip of coffee and smiled at Steph knowingly. "You're gonna get in."

Steph could even hear the period in Debra's voice. No buts.

Meanwhile, Jackie could feel his pen moving faster across the page as his ideas gained momentum. There were no more TV noises in the background, since Terry had gone off to Eduardo's house, and Jackie now had the luxury of complete concentration.

So that's how I almost started a war with a feminist club, almost lost my best friend, and almost became my town's first male beauty queen, all in one week. Reflecting on it all, I learned that the truth is, "working hard" and "being a nice guy" are super vague ideas. There's so much more to it than that. There needs to be passion. This past week, I also almost found what that passion was. I like making things change and watching things improve. I know that, since I didn't win, maybe I wasn't able to change the social climate of my town all at once. But I did see some changes in some people, and that's where change starts. I say that I "almost" found my passion, because I know that change is also a super vague idea. I don't know exactly what I love just yet, but more than anything, I want to find out. I want to watch myself change and improve and become truly devoted to something. I want to do that at your university.

Jackie sat back and stared at the new words on his paper. For the first time, he felt like he was actually on his way to a really kick-ass essay. He might have continued staring at the draft of his essay all day long, had a loud slamming of his front door not snapped his head to attention.

"Guess what you're looking at!" shouted Logan as he burst into the living room.

"A really good friend that I've taken for granted for far too long?" Jackie tried, giving Logan a small shrug and a sheepish smile.

"Nice guess. But no," said Logan. "And, dude, you already apologized to me in front of half the town. Trust me, we're good now."

All of Jackie's facial muscles relaxed as a relieved smile overtook his face. "All right, then what am I looking at?"

Logan plopped onto the couch cushion next to Jackie and, smiling, turned his head to face him. "You're looking at NYU's newest English major! Early decision for the *win*!"

Jackie raised his arm for a high-five. "Yes!" he shouted, his exclamation punctuated by the loud slapping of their hands. "Want to go eat some convenience store ice cream on the roof to celebrate? It'll be on the house."

"You mean you'll get it taken out of your paycheck?"

Jackie smiled. He stood up from the couch. "Let's go."

As he and Logan walked toward the door to leave, Jackie realized that he had never felt this great of a level of satisfaction before. Glancing back at his completed essay draft on the couch, he thought about the past week, and how, for the first time ever, he'd experienced the feeling that came with having a real sense of purpose. And now, here was Logan, who'd just gained a new security that his dream of getting out of this town was going to be a reality. After a few seconds of silent reflection, Jackie finally said, "I guess things are about to start getting a lot better for the both of us."

"Yeah." Logan nodded as he opened the front door. "I really think they are."

Acknowledgments

First, a huge shout-out to my wonderful parents, Lola and Jeff, who have encouraged me to pursue my dream of writing ever since I was four years old and wrote my first story about a Chihuahua stealing a candy cane from a Christmas tree. Though you had to sit through all the angsty, melodramatic novels I attempted to write as a teenager, your support was unwavering.

Second, thank you to the wonderful ladies of my critique group, Nancy, Emily, and Leah. Your perspectives and attention to detail helped me so much during my revision process.

Third, thank you to my partner, Tyler, who not only built the computer I typed this novel on, but also helped me do anything mildly technologically involved in this process. Everyone knows I'm not tech savvy. (I'm just regular Savy.)

Finally, I need to thank the town of West Chester, Pennsylvania, for being a much better place to grow up than Grey Acres would have been. You also had a really fun fair every year. Sorry I never entered the pumpkin contest.

ABOUT THE AUTHOR

Savy Leiser is a graduate of Northwestern University who works as a freelance writer in Chicago. Her hobbies include losing her voice screaming at Wildcats football games, occasionally performing stand-up comedy around Chicago, and inventing new recipes that utilize buffalo sauce as the main ingredient. *The Making of a Small-Town Beauty King* is her first novel.

Made in the USA
Charleston, SC
25 May 2016